# The Best of CaféLit 14

# The Best of CaféLit 14

## an anthology

*Edited by Amanda Jones*

**Chapeltown Books**

British Library Cataloguing in Publication Data

A Record of this Publication is available from the British Library

ISBN 978-1-915762-24-5

This edition published 2025 by Chapeltown Books
Manchester, England

# Contents

# Foreword

It has been absolutely delightful to select the stories for this anthology. Thank you Gill James. The collection of around 38000 words covers all genres from life lessons to funny tales and reality to future technology. All stories are ideal to enjoy with a cuppa, and it's fun to read the drinks assigned to each one. Is it a refreshing lemonade or a dark mocha?

Stories follow seasonal themes at times too which is always interesting. Some lead to books where a series has been created and here you find a section as a taster but standing in its own right as a story.

Beautiful life changes and morals are created. Reminiscences on far-gone memories abide. Everyday occurrences go right and wrong. Job prospects change. Love blossoms and fades. Our natural world is explored. A bit of horror creeps in. Murder is found. Travel across the world with the stories and our authors. You will find the variety intriguing and will laugh out loud at some.

As you go to your favourite café why not take this book with you? A story per drink is ideal. Gazing out of the window, people watching and meeting friends can add to the mix of course. The background noise of business fades away, the birdsong becomes more apparent as you relax. Let yourself be transported for a while.

Reading and selecting involves getting to know

different writing styles and the flavour of the words. Each author writes in a unique way bringing their story to life.

The talent and imagination is set free.

Variety, different authors, setting, storyline and presentation are all factors in writing. Working as an editor, author and proof reader brings all of these together. Being both a participant and selector makes CaféLit is a joy to work on. Do you have a story in you? Why not submit one? See the back of the book for details.

Inspiration comes from reading as well as experiences and short stories offer such thought. They are wrapped in a crisp format with an ending a chapter doesn't always give and can be woven into longer pieces if they develop further.

Please enjoy the wonderful writing in this anthology and take some time to put your feet up with a well-earned cuppa in your favourite café or at home.

Amanda Jones

# JANUARY

# Saturday Sample: Mosaic, Dancing to Lili Marlene

**Sandra Horn**

*champagne*

Holidays. Memories for grey and rainy days when even the birds have forgotten how to sing. Well, good memories anyway; toss out the bad with the rest of the rubbish. Then there's a different kind, neither good nor bad, but rare and disquieting, bequeathed by a holiday not even the widest leap of imagination can conjure.

It began with the sort of heat that made blinking a challenge, let alone moving limbs. Thank God the hotel was air-conditioned. Not that it wearied Maisie. Three and a half, and finally released from the confines of aircraft and taxi, she jigged joyously to piped music in the cool foyer. Her comical dance was always the same, bobbing up and down and side to side like a marionette, then spinning in circles, one foot thumping the ground in a fair interpretation of a Red Indian war dance.

Little actress she is, she played to the crowd – a lively party of Japanese tourists who stood chuckling at her. Nobody would have guessed she'd been up since four-thirty that morning.

Toby nudged me. 'Check out the old guy, Dad.'

I followed his bemused gaze to a silver-haired man

also watching our little star. The strangest sensation washed over me at the enchantment radiating from his lined face. Yet there was nothing to alarm, no perversion in that still, fierce gaze. He simply looked as if he'd never set eyes on anything so magical.

But it left me wondering, what was all that about? Maisie was cute as hell dancing there in her blue polka dot sundress and raspberry crocs, but she was no Swan Lake.

The minutiae of checking in called then, and by the time we were through, there was no sign of the elderly man.

Unpacking in our room later, conversation turned to him and it turned out he'd had the same effect on my wife. 'I suppose, you know, some might find it sinister, but it wasn't like that, was it? He just looked so… oh, sad and elated all at once. Perhaps we'll see him around and he might explain. Tell you something though, no-one could look that moved without deep reason. I reckon Maisie reminds him of someone. That'll be it.'

Jean's intuition seldom let her down.

We didn't have long to wait before seeing the old-timer again. Opting for a few hours at the children's pool the next morning, we found some free sun beds and were soon taking turns with Maisie the human dynamo on a cascading water slide. It was as I was towelling off after handing over to Tess, our friend passed by with a smile and a nod, before lowering his stooped frame onto the wall close by. It was no surprise when his washed-out blue eyes fixed on Maisie.

Now our granddaughter's not what you'd call conventionally pretty, but with Mum Tess's wide, tilted eyes and pert nose, Dad's strong chin and fresh colouring, all topped off with silky white-blonde locks, it's a striking combination that draws smiles and attention wherever she goes. Despite this, her watcher's absorption was still something else.

As if aware of my scrutiny, his unguarded gaze shifted to me. It seemed ridiculous to look away, so I gave him a small salute and wandered over to where he sat in a wedge of shade beneath a faded angelica tree.

'Lovely child,' he stated without guile, pushing steel-rimmed spectacles up his long, narrow nose.

Trying to place his thick accent, I nodded proudly. 'My granddaughter. Part angel, part savage.'

He smiled, deep lines spreading like sunrays at the corners of each eye. His gaze grew rapt again as the subject of our conversation came splashing back, squealing at Toby chasing her. 'Come and say hello, honey,' I called.

Bouncing over, she let the old man shake her hand, peering up into his kind open face inquisitively, but becoming atypically subdued. Perhaps even at that tender age, children can sense another's emotion, notice tears welling in eyes.

Her new acquaintance seemed reluctant to let go

of her hand, and even more oddly, she let it lie there. It was peculiar to witness this hushed state, something normally only surrendered to in sleep. I felt tears prick behind my own eyes then. There was such trusting innocence in her gaze, it made you feel all the good in the world. To think of life eroding it broke your heart, and I think I might have sold my soul that moment to keep her that way.

'My name's Jacob,' the old man was saying gently. 'Do you have a name too?'

'Maisie. And that's my Bampy Ken.' The spell was broken as Maisie giggled up at me, smiles dancing across her cheeky features once more.

Jean called then, 'Come on, you two, we're off to explore.'

I turned to see her gathering our paraphernalia together with her quick, economical movements. At the same time, I clearly heard Maisie say, 'Writing.' It seemed a peculiar thing for her to say to the old man, but when Tess came over, sweeping us both off, it slipped from my mind. There was no hint of the shocking intensity with which it would return.

The following evening was sticky. Dining early because of Maisie's bedtime, we found the garden restaurant cooled by a keen, maquis-scented breeze. To the horizon, the waters of the bay burned fiery from setting sun the colour of a ripe apricot. An ancient boat chugged lazily through the gentle waves to anchor. To distant sounds of rigging clanging against yacht masts, we settled beneath bleached parasols, the feel-good factor of a holiday well begun wrapping around us all.

Whilst we ordered dinner, Maisie played with her current imaginary friend. This one was her dancing friend. She'd had these harmless substitutes for some time now, whenever the real article wasn't available. Their one-sided conversation was inventively enjoyed, amidst much spinning and dancing, or playing hide and seek.

Jean spotted Jacob, laboriously climbing the steps from the lower level where the children's pool still rang with shrieks and laughter. 'Let's ask him to join us. He looks so lonely.'

We're a friendly, easy-going bunch and no-one objected. But no, Jacob declined breathlessly, though clearly touched at our offer; he'd dined midday, so perhaps another time.

His eyes flitted constantly to Maisie as he spoke and when, bless her, she ran over and slipped her hand into his, clearly having taken a shine to him, he visibly struggled to control his emotions.

'There's a huge story there.' Tess shook her dark cropped head, hazel eyes sad at Jacob's narrow form disappearing into the hotel.

Over the next thankfully cooler days, we explored the old town, swam, snacked in harbourside cafes, dined sometimes in the hotel, sometimes in the nearest village or town. Sociable Maisie made friends, and when they weren't around, there was always the one from make-believe land.

From the first evening, the sound of a harmonica softly playing from someone's veranda had caught our ears. Of course it set our little dancer off, swaying to lonesome, wistful tunes, jigging to foot-tapping ones.

The verandas were set in a gentle curve that concealed occupants from neighbours. Still, it didn't take Maisie long to discover who the musician was. Darting to where the notes tripped from, they died away as she stopped to stare. A hand stretched out to hers and I tensed, ready to chase over. One never knew. Then Jacob's head emerged and he smiled and waved before retreating out of sight once more. A few more tunes, then his recital ended with Lili Marlene, to gentle applause from unseen hands on other balconies.

We became accustomed to this routine as our holiday progressed, Jacob always saving the poignant, famous tune until last.

'What is that?' Toby asked.

'Lili Marlene. It's an old German war tune. Kind of remarkable, because it was loved by all sides. Transcended all the hatred.'

Sat beside Jean on the beach just across from our hotel the next day, Maisie pointed at spidery thread veins mapping a patch of her Nan's plump leg. Jean's not self-conscious over such crumbling round the edges and gave a fat chuckle when Maisie logically announced, 'Writing, Nana.'

So all's explained, I thought – that was why Maisie had said it to Jacob. Just veins. I wish I could have been right.

Over the next few days, we bumped into the old man often, but it wasn't until the end of our first week I really got talking to him. Breakfasting outside after managing to grab the last vacant table, we saw him appear with his slow and heavy step that always reminded me of an invalid's. He stopped, looking around as if for an unoccupied seat.

From the first, once Maisie had scoffed her food down, the little madam had kicked off to go to the play park close by, so in the absence of a naughty step to deflect a meltdown tantrum, we took turns to take her. Toby was on duty this time, and I waved Jacob over, indicating the empty seat. 'Park yourself there, my friend.'

His deep brow creased briefly, before smoothing out in a smile of understanding. 'Ah, the colloquial, yes?'

'Hopeless, us Brits. Yeah, please join us for breakfast.'

Hesitantly, he did, worrying about imposing.

Mere seconds passed before he wondered in his softly-spoken way, 'Where is the child?'

While I finished my breakfast, Jean and Tess chatted to Jacob, me observing his slow smile and the way he paused thoughtfully, head slightly inclined, before answering any question.

When the girls excused themselves to join Maisie and Toby, it left us two men alone. You know how strangers meet and it's as if there's a natural conduit flowing from one to the other? That was how it was with Jacob and me.

As if we'd fallen mentally into step with each other, he instinctively solved what had been puzzling me, as if reading my mind, 'Maisie is so like my beloved daughter at that age. Here. You will see how I mean and perhaps forgive my looking since I first see her.'

Reaching into his shirt pocket, he produced a small wallet, opening it to reveal two photos. 'My wife and daughter.'

I saw a handsome woman and a young girl. Although the girl was older than Maisie, the likeness was so uncanny it made me gasp. Jean had been spot on.

Jacob nodded as if to say, now you understand, before continuing, 'And as well in her ways. All exuberance. All promise of tomorrows. When she last came here with my wife and myself, it was her birthday. It was the best time, the last of the happy times, you understand. Promise me we shall spend my birthday always here, Papa, she said. Her name was Lilian. Lili she was always to us. That is why I play Lili Marlene. For her.'

Some people talk endlessly and never say a word.

Jacob spoke potently in so few, 'I lost my wife and Lili in the war.' He sighed, a bone-weary sound, removing his spectacles and drawing a hand over his eyes as if to wipe an image away. 'Since, I come here each year to remember my promise for Lili's birthday. It is tomorrow.'

The pause seemed unstoppable. I suppose if I'd been a woman, I might have lain a compassionate hand upon his veined one lying still on the table, but men refrain from such things. My sympathy sounded poor and hollow, 'I am so sorry.'

Jacob rallied, making an obvious effort to dispel the air of melancholy that had fallen over us like ashy-grey twilight. 'And what of you? Will famous English reserve mind me asking a little?'

His gentle civility, but with a mischievous twinkle in his eye, made me grin. 'I don't mind if you ask a lot. We come from North Wales. You might know it?'

'I do. Very beautiful, is it not? Similar to my own Austrian mountains, I think.'

'I'm a teacher. History,' I volunteered, hoping for some return. I wasn't denied, though it took me to a desolate place.

'Ah, much patience,' he chuckled. 'I salute you. Myself, these old bones can no longer work, but once I possessed my own shop. It was successful. I had an eye for beauty of the unusual kind, and grand houses patronised my furnishings… ah, terrible, listen to me. You will think I am puffing out my chest.'

I heard his words, but they seemed to come from far off, because a wintry chill was numbing my mind. There was a gusty warm wind that day, catching at hats, snatching at napkins, and as Jacob raised an arm to smooth back his thin wisping hair, it blew one loose sleeve of his shirt up his skinny arm.

With acute suddenness I found myself in visions of the past, moving through Jacob's graceful emporium, past sumptuous rolls of jewel-coloured silks and brocades, only to watch the colours fade, the materials lose their sheen and grow shabby. From the street came the sound of marching jackboots. And on the window, like a wasted prayer, was a Star of David.

Jacob lowered his arm and his forearm became concealed once more, but imprinted on my mind, as indelibly as on the old man's sagging skin, was the blurred line of a serial number. And Maisie's voice came back hauntingly, 'Writing.'

The thought arrived like an unwelcome visitor before I could lock it out – of Jacob's wife and daughter, their arms marked with the same abomination.

I'd like to have had more time to get to know the man, but on that day that had lost its lustre, time was running out.

We took a boat trip to a neighbouring island the next day, not arriving back until early evening. Maisie had fallen into a pattern of scampering up to Jacob's veranda as soon as he began playing his harmonica, and there she would tirelessly dance until the poignant notes of Lili Marlene faded away.

Tonight, however, the sequence was broken, for the old tune came first. Getting dressed for supper, I peered at the imp through vertical blinds on our half-open patio doors. Her dancing never failed to lift my spirits, which had been subdued since yesterday.

There she was dancing with her pretend friend, turning round and round, both arms held out, as if holding another's hands. My own hands fell away from the belt buckle I was fastening, and I sucked in a sharp breath, before I realised it must be a trick of light on glass, that the taller version of Maisie dancing with her was simply a mirror image projected by the sun.

Grinning and shaking my head hopelessly at myself, I finished dressing, listening to the dying notes of Lili Marlene. Jean, smelling of aftersun, drew the blinds back and slid the doors fully open. 'Will you listen to that child now? Standing up by Jacob's veranda and singing "Happy Birthday", she is. Whatever next. You don't suppose it's Jacob's birthday, do you? We must ask.'

I turned away, swallowing a sudden lump in my throat, knowing Maisie must have been singing it with Jacob for Lilian. I'd kept his story to myself. It wasn't one for a carefree family holiday. I'd tell Jean when we got home.

Passing Jacob's room later as we were all going out, his door stood ajar. Knowing no-one would object, I said, 'Hang on and I'll see if he'd like to eat with us.'

I tapped on the door and it swung inwards to reveal the wiry, olive-skinned hotel manager and two young raven-haired maids. He seemed to be supervising them and all were grim-faced. Wardrobe doors and drawers hung open. A single bed lay strewn with items of clothing and a small suitcase.

The staff all turned toward us and the manager put on his efficient face. 'Ah, good evening. The Curtis family. One moment, please.' He crisply instructed the maids in their own language before joining us in the corridor. 'You were acquainted with the occupant?' His past tense gravity made something leaden settle in the pit of my stomach.

I glanced at the door number eagerly. Had we stopped at the wrong one? But, no.

'What's happened?' Tess asked the question stuck in my throat.

The manager forgot his professional face and looked genuinely distressed. 'The gentleman passed away some time during the night.'

Only vaguely I heard the others gasp, because I was hearing Jacob's harmonica playing in my head, as it had only a short while ago.

'Jacob?' My voice sounded thin and tinny.

'Jacob Hendel. Yes, I regret.'

Jean tucked her arm through mine, and I hung onto it as the world fragmented and hazily reformed. I could feel sweat filming over my shoulder blades. 'But I saw, heard… only just now…' My voice trailed off.

I tried to pull myself together with rational thoughts – Jacob's death had to be expected. He was an old fella, after all, and hadn't looked too perky. Game over and all that trite stuff. But my vision blurred and all I wanted was to steal away and be somewhere alone. Somewhere to gather my thoughts and send out a wish to our friend.

From behind me, Maisie's shrill objecting voice cut into the silence, 'No, no, no.'

I turned to see her back in Jacob's room, resolutely clutching something to her chest. She was standing beside a small wooden table. On its top lay sunglasses, suncream, and that familiar harmonica. No doubt the photograph frame she was refusing to return to the maid had also stood there before she'd grabbed it.

Nimbly avoiding the girl, she dashed over to me, face aglow. 'Look. See.'

Shakily, I hunkered down so my eyes were level with hers, and together we gazed at the grainy photograph set in the frame. Lilian gazed back at us.

Cradling the photo to her as she did her favourite doll, Maisie said solemnly, 'My dancing friend. Gone home with Papa Jacob now.'

In a sleepy, tree-lined square in the old part of town, a tiny church rests serenely. Tomorrow I would take a wander down there and sit in the cool silence in one of the hand-carved pews. There I would send out my wish to Jacob, God speed, my friend. God speed both of you.

After that I would pass behind the church into the airless labyrinth of alleyways where a shabby store leans, selling all kinds of music. If I was lucky, high on a shelf, gathering dust, I might find Lili Marlene.

Something to play on a grey and rainy day to remind us how fortunate we are.

# FEBRUARY

# All Change

Jane Mooney

***milky instant coffee***

I struggled to wake from the fog of a deep sleep. My limbs felt heavy. My mouth was dry and sticky, like peanut butter. The beginnings of a headache were tickling around my temples and the bright lights in the train carriage hurt my eyes. As I reached for my bag to look for the paracetamol there was an announcement over the tannoy.

*We will shortly be arriving in Plymouth. This train terminates here. All change.*

Panic clenched my chest. How was I in Plymouth? I was supposed to be in Doncaster! I racked my brains. We'd been out in York celebrating Joan's retirement. We'd done *Bottomless Brunch,* which had seemed like a good idea at the time. For an all-inclusive price of £35 we got something to eat and as much as we could drink in two hours. I'm a lightweight when it comes to drinking, so I liked the idea that it was time limited. I figured I couldn't do too much damage in two hours.

Well, it hadn't quite worked like that. After the limited time, we'd gone on to another bar, then another. I had a vague memory of drunken, giggly hugs at York station before we'd all gone our separate ways.

And here I was in Plymouth. The train slowed to a screeching halt, and I took my purse out of my pocket to see how much cash I'd got. £3.75. And I'd left my bank cards at home so I didn't overspend. Oh Gosh, how on Earth was I going to get back to Doncaster?

The train pulled out of the station, leaving me on a windy, deserted platform. I thought there'd be someone to ask, but it was the middle of the night and there was no-one around so I made my way through a subway and into the ticket hall. The doors were locked. I couldn't get out.

I sat down heavily on a bench with a lump in my throat. How could I have been so careless? The first time I'd been out since I'd lost Geoff and I'd managed to get on the wrong train AND to fall asleep as well! I pulled my cardi tight around my shoulders and cursed my friend Moira who'd persuaded me to wear this stupid flimsy dress.

Despite the cold I must have fallen asleep because I woke suddenly when a group of shouting lads emerged from the subway. They were about 16 or 17, just a little younger than my girls. I shrank into the seat hoping they wouldn't notice me. At first, they were too busy showing off to each other, but then they spotted me.

'Hey! What we got here?' said one.

'Looks like she's 'ad a rough night!' said another.

'Let's see if she's got anything worth 'aving,' said

the biggest of the boys as he reached for my handbag.

He grabbed one handle. I had hold of the other, and as he tugged the bag towards him, he pulled me out of my seat.

'Give it here!' I yelled, yanking it back in a ridiculous tug of war.

'Why should I?' he whispered quietly.

He moved closer, so close I could smell the alcohol and cannabis on his breath. I tasted fear, sharp and metallic in the back of my mouth, but I wasn't going to let him have my bag. The rest of them were closing in, like a pack of hyenas in a TV documentary. I looked around for an escape route and noticed that the doors at the front of the station were now open. With a well-aimed kick to his shins, I was able to grab the bag and run for the open doors. I ran out of the station and kept on running.

When I eventually stopped, I was out of breath and shaking, but it didn't look as if the boys had followed me. The air was chilly and the sky was all shades of pink and purple. There was a café on the corner, lights on, windows steamed up. It looked very welcoming.

As I pushed the door open the hot aroma of frying bacon hit me, and my mouth started to water. It was crowded. Mostly workmen in overalls. The odd businessman in a smart suit. No women other than a harassed looking waitress behind the counter.

I was still shaking, and my head was throbbing. I

took a few deep breaths to steady myself before stepping forward.

'What can I do for you love?' the waitress asked.

'Just a coffee please.'

She steamed the milk and poured it onto instant coffee granules.

'Nothing else love?'

Studying the menu which hung above the counter, I checked my pockets for further stashes of cash, hoping I had enough for a bacon sandwich. Nothing.

'Maybe a glass of water,' I said. At least that should help the hangover.

I carried my drinks to a table by the window and leaned my head against the damp glass. The coolness felt good against my pounding head. I heaped two spoonfuls of sugar into the mug and stirred it slowly. After the first scalding hot, milky sip I began to think straight, and to wonder how on Earth I was going to get home?

Always one for a good list, I pulled a notebook and pen out of my bag and started to jot down ideas:

1. *Hitchhike.*

But it's a long way from Plymouth to Yorkshire, and I might get murdered.

2. *Beg, steal, or borrow the money for the train ticket.*

But I'm too shy to beg, too honest to steal and I didn't know anyone in Plymouth to borrow from.

3. *Get a job and earn the money for the ticket.*

But doing what?

4. *Phone Moira and see if she can come and pick me up.*

I'd never live that down.

5. …

I'd run out of ideas. I reckoned phoning Moira might be the best bet, and in any case, I should let her know I wouldn't be coming into work. I pulled my phone out of my pocket, but the screen was black. Completely dead. Of course! I'd been using Google maps to find my way around York and that always eats up the battery. I delved into my bag to see if I had my charger with me. Nope. Well so much for that idea.

Behind the counter the waitress was yelling into her phone. She threw it down, tore off her apron, and stormed angrily out of the door. Through the window I could see her shaking a cigarette carton. It was empty. She leaned back against the window. Then I remembered I had Moira's fags in my bag from yesterday so I went outside and offered them to the her.

'Thanks love, you've no idea how much I need this!' She put the cigarette between her lips and lit it. She took a deep pull and breathed out slowly.

'That's better,' she said. 'The girl who helps with

lunches has blobbed again. It's the third time in a fortnight, and I could really do without it today. I need to get everything cleaned up quickly 'cos it's my little boy's school assembly.'

'Can I help?'

'Are you a waitress?'

'No, I'm a lab assistant,' I said. 'But I know how to wash up and I've nothing else to do today?'

'You sure?'

'Sure I'm sure,' I said. 'And if you've got an iPhone charger so I can charge my phone I'm even more sure!'

'Well, you're on Missus,' said the waitress. 'I'm Tash.'

'Liz.'

'Well Liz, you might just be a life saver today.'

We went inside and Tash pointed to a phone charger in the corner of the kitchen, then gave me an apron to wear and showed me where I could lock my bag and coat in the storeroom. The first job was to clear the tables, which were stacked high with greasy plates from the breakfast rush. I dumped them in the sink and spent the next twenty minutes up to my elbows in hot, soapy bubbliness. This was very different to washing test tubes and flasks. Then there were salads to wash and vegetables to prepare.

We chatted as we worked. Tash told me about her little boy, eight years old and thought he was the next David Beckham. I told her about my two girls, off at university and almost grown up. At lunchtime Tash took the orders and did the cooking and I delivered the plates of food and cleared the tables. I couldn't believe how many people came through the door of this small café in a couple of hours. There were takeaway orders too, office workers coming in for sandwiches or burgers to take back to their desks. Around two it quietened off and Tash handed me a cup of coffee.

'Something to eat?' she asked. 'There's some meat and potato pie left.'

I attacked the pie with gusto.

'You look like you haven't eaten in days,' Tash joked.

My face burned when I told her my last meal had been 'brunch' in York yesterday, and there'd been a lot more drinking than eating involved. I told her about falling asleep on the train, and ending up in Plymouth, and the lads who tried to nick my bag at the train station.

'Oh blimey,' said Tash, 'and I thought I was having a bad day.'

'Well, it got better after I came in here.' I said. 'I've really enjoyed helping you, especially the banter with the customers. You don't get that in the hospital lab.'

'Why didn't you just get a train straight back?'

'No money,' I said with a shrug.

Tash went to the till and pulled out six £20 notes which she put down on the table in front of me.

'Oh, Tash, I wasn't asking for money. I wanted to help you out.'

'You've earned it. I'd never have got through today if you hadn't been here to help.'

I looked at the notes on the table. It was probably enough to get me home. Problem solved.

'How about staying on?' asked Tash. 'I was going to kick my assistant into touch. She keeps letting me down. So I can offer you regular work, five days a week. What do you say?'

I was about to say, *No. I can't. I live in Doncaster.* Then I thought, *Why not?* What was keeping me in Doncaster now the girls were at university? My job had felt like a dead end for the last ten years. Perhaps it was time for a complete change.

'Pass me my phone,' I said. I dialled Moira's number.

# Avril

## Judith Skilleter

*coffee*

Avril loves cooking but she loves recipe books much much more. She has so many of them that her bookcase is overflowing. The problem is that Avril enjoys cookery programmes and she inevitably buys the book that goes along with that particular series and it is perusing these books that gives Avril the most pleasure. Avril is a decent enough cook but she cooks very carefully so as not to make a mess on her precious cookbooks. Some books she uses more than others but in some books she returns to the same recipe time and time again. An example of a book that Avril uses a lot is *Delia's Cakes.* Avril has the waistline of a keen baker; there is not much that Avril likes better than a new cake emerging from the oven. But an example of a recipe book used for one recipe only would be a Gino D'Acampo whose caramelised onion meatballs are a great favourite of Avril and her nieces and nephews.

Avril has no children; she has never married and it is some years since she had any relationship with a man let alone have a serious relationship. Her nieces and nephews say her relationships are with her cook books, the way she tenderly turns over the pages and runs her finger tips over the colour plates, the way her eyes open and moisten when she finds a particularly special recipe is worthy of any close relationship with a man or indeed a women. Cookery books are always her choice for her bedtime reading.

But Avril is neither lonely nor alone; she has close relationships with all her nieces and nephews and she tells them that had she had children of her own she hoped they would be exactly like them. This love is reciprocated. – they adore Auntie Av.

Has she got cooking favourites? Yes and no. It depends on circumstances, it depends on how she is feeling and it depends on the weather. There are days when the humour of Jamie Oliver cheers her up no end, there are days when her need for a nice piece of fish leads to her looking through her many books by Rick Stein and for normal days when she wants to jazz up something ordinary she will always look to The Hairy Bikers. She does have a great fondness for Raymond Blanc but his recipes are sometimes too fancy for what she needs. One day she will treat herself to a night at Le Manoir aux Quat'Saisons. She doesn't know yet but her nieces and nephews have booked her into Le Manoir for her next birthday.

Avril's first cookbook was a BeRo book inherited from her mother. It was a thin paperback with a young girl on the front and back cover showing the world how to make cakes and biscuits. This book has been well used over the years; its cover has been reinforced and fixed back in place many times. But it gave Avril the solid baking grounding she needed – nothing too tricky and nothing needing too many ingredients.

Avril went through a phase of enjoying Indian food and bought Madhur Jaffrey's books. Nowadays her elderly digestion cannot take spicy food and it is with regret that her Indian recipe books have been put on the unreachable top shelf of her cookery library. Also up there with the Jaffreys are her books without colour illustrations. Avril likes to see what her cooking project will look like and she gets a thrill if her finished object is like the picture in the book. Avril reckons that her Chinese cookbooks will be the next selection relegated to the top shelf – too fiddley with too many ingredients that are not easy to get.

But to her total and absolute horror the beloved nieces and nephews bought her a swanky and complicated Air Fryer for her Christmas present. She was polite and said, 'Thank you very much – I will enjoy learning to use it and I look forward to making things in it that you all will enjoy. As ever you are all very lovely.' But when they all left she looked at this enormous square object taking up a lot of room on her kitchen surfaces and shook her head in dismay. 'What on earth am I going to do with you?' she said to it. It was too heavy for her to lift or lug about so she would not be able to put it in a cupboard and forget about in between niece and nephew visits. Even if she could lift it there was no room in her kitchen cupboards for something of that size.

She pulled out the two drawers and wondered how these shoe box lookalikes could produce decent food. Yes she had seen cooks raving about them on TV but where was the very useful window where you could check how things were progressing? Surely if you pulled open the drawer too early everything would sink – especially Yorkshire puddings. And she thought with horror about the impact of sneaky and early looks would have on her cakes.

Avril went to bed in a very despondent frame of mind. As she climbed the stairs she shook her head and wondered how she could deal with the Dalek lookalike without upsetting her beloved relatives. The Air Fryer was not the first of well-meant but unwanted presents from the nephews and nieces. Ten years ago they bought her a top of the range micro wave oven. It sat on her kitchen surface for two months until Avril realised it was only being used for warming milk and cooking frozen peas. It is now in the cupboard under the stairs next to the very fancy food mixer and food processor not unlike the one used by Nigella Lawson. It was a beautiful machine, all grey stainless steel, but Avril continues to use her thirty year old hand held mixer which is light weight, slots into a drawer and does not need close attention. A George Forman grill was never used and it went off to the local hospice shop and the sandwich maker went to the tip because Avril got fed up with all the cleaning and scraping it needed after one use.

Avril enjoys good coffee and would like a coffee making machine. But she does not dare to suggest this to the nephews and nieces – they would buy her a top of the range, multi-purpose, many levered gadget – probably with an introduction to George Clooney as a bonus – but all she wants is a simple device that did not offer ten or more choices of coffee. Three would do – latte, decaffeinated espresso and Americano.

Next morning Avril got up as usual and went downstairs for her morning cup of tea. She was taken aback by the size of the Air Fryer on her kitchen surface. *It has grown overnight*, she thought to herself, a*nd it looks even more threatening and menacing sitting there in all its polished glory. This will just not do.*

But a plan was taking shape in her mind.

Next door had a twelve year old son who did occasional errands for Avril – she paid him of course. Next time she heard him in the garden she shouted over the fence, 'Max may I borrow you for a moment. Just check that it's OK with your mum first though.'

She then heard Max's mum calling back to her, 'Are you alright Avril – what can we do?'

'I need some lifting doing if that's OK.'

'Max is on his way but don't give him as much money as you did last time – he will only buy rubbish with it.'

'OK,' lied Avril.

Max came in and was led to the cupboard under the stairs. 'I need some rearranging Max,' said Avril, 'and sorting for the tip.'

Max nodded.

Half an hour later the two suitcases filled with tablecloths and blankets were in the spare room ready to be sorted for either a charity shop or the tip. Avril's set of bowling balls was next to the front door ready to be taken to the local bowls club – Avril hadn't played for years. A box of videos was also at the front door ready for the tip – 'Why on earth do you still have these? The video player went years ago' – and a cassette recorder and two shoeboxes of cassettes joined the videos at the front door. All sorts came out of that cupboard, never to go back. Avril gave it a good sweep out before putting back the microwave, the food processer and mixer and she made sure that there was plenty of room for the Air Fryer which she and Max eased in. 'And there's still room for next year's present,' said Avril to a bemused Max.

Max agreed, of course he did; he went home with a tenner.

# MARCH

# Too Close

## Elise Glassman

### *Pisco sour*

How had they ended up in this strange little town? Well, their friends had raved about it. A must-see, they insisted, with glorious mineral springs and an adorable brewery. She'd been doubtful. She and her partner were city people, they went to museums and shows, not on rural vacations, and certainly not the germy soup of a public Southwestern hot springs. But the friends, early Microsoft retirees, were persuasive. They travelled well, knew the best beaches in Costa Rica, whose Mediterranean yacht had an available cabin, which swanky supper club might seat two more. Saying no might put a strain on future socializing, mark them somehow as inferior friends, so they agreed: they'd make a quick stop, spend the night, post photos, keep it moving.

They arrived on a windy afternoon, too early to check into their Airbnb, so she drove their rental car along a two-lane street through town, took a dogleg to the right and parked beside a river.

'Look, it's the Rio Grande.'

'The Rio Grande,' her partner echoed. 'Wow.'

They got out into warm sun, the grass smelling of dry hay, the river water rippling along low vegetal banks. She felt a small thrill. It was a legendary river, wasn't it?

At least it was in the black-and-white Westerns she watched as a kid with her dad; Hollywood fantasies of a time and place she knew now had never really existed, of virtuous, strong-jawed lawmen and hardy white women and freckle-faced kids learning life lessons.

Finally, check-in time. They gazed out at the Airbnb, an elderly stucco cottage with a sagging porch. 'Jeez, I hope it's norm core,' she said doubtfully.

'Maybe.' He lifted luggage and groceries from the trunk while she retrieved the keys. Inside, the house smelled okay and passed the fingertip test. They walked through a bright yellow kitchen and past a narrow bathroom. He hefted her suitcase into the larger bedroom and dragged his down the hall to a smaller one. They hadn't slept together much on this trip, due to snoring (his) and insomniac restlessness (hers). She missed him, missed his adjacent warmth. But the chainsaw rattle of his sinuses always drove her away.

Her stomach growled so she went to the kitchen to evaluate the snack situation and found him studying the house binder, the four single-space pages devoted to tub operations. 'I guess we should try a soak?' She'd never gotten in a mineral tub before, and this wasn't an inexpensive rental. She wanted to get her money's worth.

'I guess so.'

So they performed the complex series of steps, each showering, then donning bathing suits, then opening the mineral tub valve to rinse, warm, and fill the chunky concrete tub. 'It's definitely a homemade job,' she smirked, sinking into steaming water up to her chin.

'For sure homemade,' he agreed.

Clouds had scudded in overhead, obscuring the weak winter sun. She tried to enjoy the delicious warmth, to forget about the sad little back yard, the cracked patio and shrivelled plants. Then, frowning, she opened her eyes. 'What is that sound?' It was a constant, breathy sigh, like the thrum of crickets. A sound she associated with Midwestern summers and her grandfather's singed lawn.

'What is it?' He was looking around, too.

'It sounds like doves? Cooing?' She squinted, but all she saw was leafless branches.

'It does sound like doves.'

Then where the hell were they? And was she a terrible person, finding such an objectively poetic sound annoying? The sound felt oppressive. It felt like beady little eyes were observing them. Waiting for – well, what? It wasn't like there were vultures up there circling.

The friends had raptured about leisurely soaks but they stayed in just long enough to braise their goose flesh, then dashed inside to shower again and shiver by the gas fireplace.

For dinner, he offered to cook tostadas with frozen Hatch chiles they'd bought in Las Cruces. Her job was defrosting, and she watched the frozen logs circle in the microwave, waiting for the tender moment between done and explosion. 'Was it me or was the shower not very hot?'

'Not hot,' he confirmed, turning on the stove burner. 'Or maybe we were just really cold.'

Opening the microwave, she poked at a rigid chili. 'These are still frozen. Can we put 'em in the hot pan and I'll find another pan for tortillas?'

'Throw 'em in the hot pan,' he said agreeably.

While the chiles warmed, she searched the cupboards for a second pan but found only mismatched plates, earthenware bowls and mugs and a cutting board. Whatever. She'd wait and wash out his pan when he was done. But the water went abruptly cold as she started to rinse. 'Dang it.'

Again they consulted the binder. 'Please Be Gentle!!' the hot water section was titled. Reading over her shoulder, the dense pages of instructions and photos, he sighed, 'Oh, dang.'

'I want all the beer,' she said.

'Oh. we're getting all the beer.'

In the end they'd thrown the chili pan in the sink and headed to the brewery. The friends had enthused about it too, the crisp beers, the fire pit, the camaraderie with locals. But the cavernous space reminded her of a VFW hall. A moustached bartender was in deep conversation with a woman in a biker vest and cap. The wooden booths sat mostly empty, the tables speckled with dried beer glass rings.

The bartender leaned out of his conversation. 'What can I get ya?'

'One IPA, one lager,' she requested. 'And pizza?' Hot pizza might salvage things.

'You can order from Geppetto's,' he said, explaining the brewery had no kitchen but restaurants in town delivered.

Now the other customers were looking at them. She felt anxious sweat prickle her armpits. They took their beer to the front patio to enjoy the waning sun. 'Should I order a pizza?' he asked and she snapped, 'Order a pizza. Please.'

Sighing, he showed her his phone screen. Closed. The nearby Mexican restaurant, also closed. She sipped her beer. It was crisp and quite hoppy. 'Did I get your IPA?'

'Did you?' He handed her his glass.

She sipped his, tasted the sinus punch of hops, slammed it down so hard the beer slopped out.

'Seriously. Is everything in this town a pretend version of the real thing?'

'You don't need to fix everything,' he said, wiping the spill, but they both knew he was wrong.

The next morning they soaked again in the tub. It was a warmer day. Nearby a saw buzzed, but its whine did not drown out the ominous cooing. Dripping, she climbed out of the tub. 'Where are those damn birds?' Nothing in the yard, the thicket of weeds with irrigation hoses coiled in a corner, seemed capable of sustaining life. Ignoring his feeble consolations (where are they? it's so strange) she went inside, thrust alternate limbs into the needling cold shower, dressed, shoved aside greasy dishes, and made coffee with Dunkin Donut grounds she'd discovered last night in her cupboard searches.

Pouring fragrant coffee into mugs, she yelled out the back door, 'There's coffee. I'm going for a walk.'

He was already towelling off. 'I'm coming,' he yelled, even though she stood mere feet away.

At the curb, they paused to inspect the rental car. It had survived the night with no visible dings. In fact, it glittered like a spangle among old buttons. No one needed to see the California plates to know it didn't belong. 'You hungry? I might have a granola bar in the glove compartment.' Dinner last night had been gas station fare: pistachio brittle, Miller Lite, and Cool Ranch Doritos with soggy chiles.

'Are you hungry?' he countered.

She shrugged. 'I'll eat in Albuquerque.'

So they walked down the main road, passing closed cafes and shuttered art studios and an unshaven guy in a gravel lot, inflating a bicycle tire with a hand pump. At the park by the Rio Grande, her partner clambered around on the rocks while she sipped coffee and took pictures with her phone.

'Whoa. The sky is amazing.' Her phone's filter converted the river and the rocky hills and the cloud-streaked sky into a stark, gorgeous landscape.

'Livin' the dream, baby!' The unshaven guy flew by on his bicycle.

'Livin' the dream!' her partner screamed back, flashing two thumbs up.

They watched the cyclist continue, going the wrong way on the road out of town. 'That sure seems like a metaphor,' she said.

Laughing, he returned to the sidewalk and grabbed his mug. 'The whole place is a metaphor.'

It was almost checkout time so they started the walk back on a side street, the sidewalk petering out onto parking spots, each occupied by a shiny car with out-of-state plates. 'I guess we're not the only tourists in town,' she mused.

The cars sat outside a grey, ranch-style building. A lacquered sign, set in a bed of smooth rocks, read, Rio Grande Hot Springs Hotel. Two people in Lycra and fresh sneakers emerged, laughing and sipping from Starbucks cups. '*Amazing*,' one said, and the other echoed, '*Amazing*,' and they climbed into a gleaming SUV.

As it eased away, a flier rustled in the dry gutter. She picked it up. *Deluxe rooms! Private mineral springs tubs! Four-star dining! Ask about off season rates*. 'I bet they have hot water.' She said it before he could, daring him to question that for the same money or less they could have had hot water and a private tub and beer that tasted of malt and sunshine. Had the friends stayed at this tucked-away jewel? How had she missed it? What was she going to tell them?

He'd continued his leisurely saunter, already half a block ahead. She hurried to catch up and then, hearing him humming cheerfully, speed-walked past him. She was so angry with him for not being angry, for not hating the sad house, the ineffectual water heater, the ill-furnished kitchen, the binder novella of detail and despair, the tub with its skein of pink mould.

Then he was running past her, coffee spilling from his mug, puffs of dust kicking up from his sneakered feet. By the time she caught up he was at the house, tub valve open, stripping off his shirt.

'You go ahead,' she said, when he looked at her, chest heaving. 'I'm going to figure out how to wash dishes.' The binder had a long list of check-out tasks. Could she heat tap water on the stove? Run water through the coffee maker?

'We could wash 'em here.' Grimacing, he pointed at the tub, at the steaming, ankle-deep water.

It wasn't the worst idea.

Later, sitting on a sunny patio with a small-batch mezcal, she agonized over her Airbnb review. Almost nothing had worked. And yet they'd had an okay time. She'd never forget the weird brewery and dinner of chips and The Champagne of Beers. In the end she posted four-point-five stars and sent the host a private note about the water heater. He immediately messaged back, mentioning the binder, the need to care for the old house, his proximity(??). *I was next door all day. I'd have come right over.*

She hadn't known he was so close. But wasn't the whole point to not be close? What was he even doing next door? Had he heard them cursing, yelling, beating the branches trying to find the source of the goddamned cooing? The hotel would have been the sensible choice. The choice their friends had likely made, their car snugged up to its shiny siblings, dinner on matching china, pleasant soaks in a varnished wood tub, no invisible, sinister doves.

It was a version of their lives, themselves, that she could not quite imagine.

# Reminiscences: An Old Man's Christmas Eve Recollections

**Olof Laamanen**

***mulled wine***

It's Christmas Eve, 2022.

The whole family is gathered in our house just outside Helsinki. Outside, it's bitterly cold, pitch black and a howling snowstorm rattles the windows. Inside, it's calm, warm from the logs crackling in the open fireplace, and the flickering home-cast candles on the Christmas tree's branches have turned the room into an enchanted realm.

The air is filled with the fragrance of the freshly cut fir's resin mixed with the softer scent of sugar melted over burning brandy – my father's teachings of how to make the perfect *glögg* put into practice a while ago.

Stephanie relaxes in her easy chair, sending me glances of love; our daughters and their spouses are seated around the sofa table, steaming cups of freshly brewed glögg in their hands.

The grandchildren, busy unpacking their presents, sprawl on the floor, sweets within easy reach, and each surrounded by a heap of torn Christmas paper and empty cartons.

Magic no other evening can come even close to.

Luxuriating in the cosy family scene, my heart fills

with that warm feeling of satisfaction associated with plans fulfilled and the knowledge I had made other people happy.

My old man's eyes mist over, but within the haze, a long-forgotten image from my youth appears for a fleeting moment; the present dissolves, and I'm transported to another room and another era.

It's 1962; I'm seventeen, and it's my first Christmas Eve with Anne at my side. It is also the last one. That, however, is still hidden in the swirling mists of the future.

She's my first teenage love. We met at a party the previous spring, and instant attraction blossomed. Our relationship grew in strength over the summer, and during the autumn, it became all-consuming. I could think of nothing but her. My grades slipped, and my parents, who hadn't yet met her, became worried and wanted me to see a doctor.

Had they never experienced love as teenagers?

Anne's Christmas visit to my home was her coming out; I hoped she'd be accepted as a future family member.

She was marvellous. Sitting sedately still, clothed in a blue silken dress, with a modishly short bob haircut and cheeks displaying the unique lustre of a teenage girl in love. With wings and a halo, she would have been indistinguishable from an angel in a Raphael painting. My love was limitless, and that picture of her became forever imprinted on my heart.

All my hopes for the evening were fulfilled. My parents were enchanted by her and expressed gratitude for gaining such a delightful new acquaintance. I saw an engagement the coming midsummer as a distinct possibility.

Throughout the following winter and spring, Anne and I were busy wrapping up our twelve school years. Passing the matriculation exams with good marks was all-important; those marks were our keys to the future. She wanted to become a nurse, while I aimed to be an engineer.

We could spare little time and energy for our relationship, but our love thrived. During our sparse hours together, we spun grand plans for the future, building all those castles among the clouds inherent to teenagers. Villas, summer cottages, cars, and voyages dominated, but all the children we would have was a recurring subject. I told Anne I wanted three, and she countered with a teasing, 'Why not half a dozen?'

How we should finance our dreams didn't worry us. Such earthly problems we would solve when we faced them.

The future was ours, and life was great.

Time passed quickly, and with the exams behind us and school soon ending, we were getting ready for a summer with a particular shimmer, the last one with childhood freedom. In September, the Nurse Institute awaited Anne; a month later, I'd join the army for my eleven-month stint. In the autumn of next year, we'd be grown-ups. Free to take control of our lives, but without ever again having the luxury of three months of freely disposable time.

Determined to make the most of this unique summer, we busily jotted lists of everything we would do. First on my list was a midsummer engagement.

The day after school ended, I knocked on Anne's door. Our magic summer was about to begin.

Her mother opened. 'You're too late; Anne left for the airport two hours ago.' Looking ill at ease, she quickly added, 'Let's hope three weeks of Spanish sun will do her some good. She, for sure, needs to regain her strength after all the exams.'

Three weeks abroad?

Without giving me a single word of warning.

And in Spain!

Where girls bathe topless and consort freely with eager local men, capable of seducing any Nordic girl within an hour, if you can rely on the papers.

A searing feeling of betrayal devoured my heart. The mother's shamefaced mien had revealed the truth; she knew I had been left in the dark.

But why?

Devils of jealousy attacked me. Did Anne want to end our relationship but didn't dare to say so?

Is this how girls behave when they no longer love you?

All the outrageous theories a hurt and jealous

young man could dream up whirled through my brain. Wild speculations of her escaping to join a secret lover alternated with more plausible ones.

Maybe it was a surprise end-of-school gift by her parents, giving her no time to warn me? 'Here are your tickets. The plane leaves in three hours; start packing.'

Did they fear I would make their precious daughter pregnant and thought it best to separate us?

Would serve them right if she came home from Spain knocked up by some dago!

My summer was thoroughly spoiled. Anne and her betrayal tormented my mind continuously. Images of her kept popping up in the middle of my studies, sometimes in her angel-like Christmas outfit, but more often, in only the bottom half of a bikini. I had never seen her that lightly clothed, but my imagination knew no limits.

The entry exams to the Technical University proved to be a push-over, but I felt only satisfaction, no joy. It was a milestone I had planned to celebrate with Anne.

The midsummer festivities loomed only a week later. All spring, I had looked forward to that as the right time for Anne and me to announce our engagement. Now, the event threatened to become utterly dismal. Having to watch all the happy couples dancing in the midnight half-dusk would only worsen the pain of Anne's treachery. In desperation,

I accepted a friend's invitation to join his 'Solstice Party'. There, I at least wouldn't be alone.

However, when the magic midnight of the year's shortest night approached, I was lonelier than ever, sitting alone in the empty dining hall. Everyone else danced on the terrace outside.

Suddenly, the door flew open, and two people entered. My host all smiles. 'Cheer up! Your great love is back from Spain! Just in time for a midnight kiss.'

Behind him, Anne smiled shyly.

She was as angel-like as before but now also deliciously tanned and more alluring than ever.

The sight of her tore open all my wounds.

Angel-like had overtones of betrayal, and her enticing colour made me think of wanton exposure of breasts to ogling Latinos.

Weeks of suppressed bitterness burst forth, 'She's not my great love. No great love disappears to Spain without telling me first.'

Anne looked like I had slapped her, spun around, and ran from the room.

We never met again. Too hurt and too proud to admit I had been overly hasty, I avoided her during the summer, and while I was in the army, she and her parents emigrated to America.

Still, I couldn't forget her; she remained an open wound in my soul and a constant ache in my conscience.

Why had she disappeared without warning me?

What if I had given her a chance to explain herself?

Had I hurt an innocent person by letting my wounded ego have the best of me that midsummer night?

Questions begging for answers I'd never get.

Two years passed. My studies proceeded well, but not my personal life. I met fascinating and attractive girls and even dated some of them. But none measured up to the idealized Anne in my mind.

Then I met Steph. A young woman who shared my interests in literature and long walks. After a year of shared outdoor days, discussion evenings, or moments of togetherness over a coffee, she became a permanent part of my life.

Done with our studies, we married. During the busy years when we built our life together and raised our kids, Anne finally faded from my memory.

But tonight, six decennials after that one and only Christmas Eve, she once again sat before me in the candles' flickering light for a fleeting second. Eternally innocent, dressed in silky blue, eyes sparkling, and a halo stylishly askew over her head.

Was she thinking of me at that moment?

Nostalgia overwhelms me. What if I hadn't rejected her? Would I now be a contented grandfather with her at my side and our children and grandchildren around us? – Children never born.

Dear Anne, do you, wherever you might be, ever think of me? Do you reflect on what could have been hadn't I given in to my anger that night more than half a century ago?

I turn my eyes back to my family. Life had become great even without Anne.

# APRIL

# La Bella Luna

**Kate Durrant**

### *spring water*

'I'm going to paint my toenails black,' she says as she reclines against multiple pillows.

One hand uncomfortably stretched away from her body holding the phone, allowing me a glimpse of her distended stomach and her pregnant chins.

The other idly cradling her unborn baby.

I think of 1992 when she was born and the faded, much photocopied *Preparing for hospital* A4 page which stated, as clearly as the worn cap-locked typewriters letters could *REMOVE YOUR NAIL VARNISH.*

'They have better ways to detect cyanosis now,' she says, reading my mind.

She passed her due date four days ago, and we chat by Messenger on the shoulder hours of the day. As I get up and she heads to bed, or I head to bed as *Morning Mum* appears on my screen.

'Do you want to talk?' I type.

'No,' she says, as firmly as only a nine month and four day pregnant woman can.

'Will he be home from work soon?' I ask. Checking my world clock, which reminds me that most of the time we don't share the same day.

She tells me he will, as a photograph of the Australian night sky slides onto my screen.

'Look at the moon Mum,' she types, reading my mind again.

We may not share the same day but we do, at least, sometimes share the same moon.

She promised me she wouldn't stay in Australia.

A clairvoyant told her that her tall, dark, handsome man would have his feet firmly planted in Irish soil.

She lied.

The clairvoyant that is, not my daughter. She didn't lie, she just fell in love.

'She's going to come today Mum,' she says, pushing herself up with difficulty, shuffling over to the microwave in her open-plan Antipodean kitchen to heat up another pad for her aching back.

As, inside her, the baby inches slowly towards the light and prepares to meet her mother.

It's 5 o'clock on one of those dark, damp nights between Halloween and Christmas that have neither rhyme nor reason.

I wander, lost, around the supermarket.

Picking up 70% off chocolate ghosts and full price gold-foil wrapped reindeer.

Trying to summon up enthusiasm for non-grandchild related activity, when the text comes in.

'We're on our way to the hospital,' I read, before bursting into tears.

I hide behind the door of the vegetable freezer in the frozen food aisle. The florets inside the packet of *picked fresh for you broccoli* softening in my hand.

I should be there.

She needs her mum.

I need my daughter.

I put the broccoli back, carelessly in with the carrots. Abandon the ghosts in my trolley, and return to my car leaving a trail of tears on the tarmac of the multi storey.

This was *not* how I planned it thirty-one years ago when I removed my nail varnish and waddled into the labour ward.

I text a friend, who sees past the lie of the smiley faced emoji.

'Coffee?' she replies.

As it happens we have marshmallow-topped hot chocolate instead.

Extra large.

She hugs me.

I cry.

'She needs me,' I tell her.

'Don't be silly,' she says, cream clinging to the slight shadow on her upper lip. 'She's in agony, she'd tell you to get lost.'

I laugh.

She misses her mum, recently gone.

I miss my daughter.

So we talk instead about the war raging on the other side of Europe, as the dead and the unborn lie silently on the table with our crumpled empty sugar sachets.

We finish our chocolate and go our separate ways.

Waving goodbye, only drowning a little.

A message comes in from sky-diving Sam, my daughter's love, about to take the biggest free-fall of his life.

'She's doing fine,' his text tells me, before he gowns up to stand at her right hand, and his mum arrives, taking over the role as publicist.

'She's amazing,' my daughter's mother-in-law types.

I know.

I pace the floor of the virtual maternity ward through the wee small hours. My path lit by the full moon, now keeping me company, having left her alone to her labour.

My phone taunts me with its silence and when it finally vibrates into the darkness, waking me from my sleepless night, my fingers fumble in their haste to accept the incoming video call.

I half cry and half laugh as she comes into view.

‘I can see the moon,’ I say, turning my phone to show her the village she used to call home. Bathed in silvery light, so bright it could be day.

I bring the phone back around to face me.

I stand still, and take a deep breath, as I search her exhausted face.

‘I can see the moon too,’ she says shyly, as she reclines against the hospital pillows.

One hand uncomfortably stretched away from her body holding the phone.

The other cradling her tiny, perfect, daughter, Luna.

# The Man on the Train

**Michael Barrington**

***a gin and tonic tall with lemon twist***

'Good morning, George.'

'And a good morning to yourself, Harry,' he replied with a smile. 'It's another beautiful day and we are still walking upright,' he quipped. It was the same remark he made every last Thursday of the month, and had been doing so for as long as Harry could remember.

'It's the usual, then.'

'Yes, thanks, Harry,' and he handed over the six pounds and ten pence through the narrow ticket office window for the round trip. It was always the same; Crawley to London Victoria station and he always took the same train, the 8:17 a.m. And you could practically set your watch that he would return on the 5:11 p.m.

'He's a very nice but strange bloke,' Harry had confided to his friend Alf, the station master, over a cup of tea. There was no train for another hour and a half. 'Never says much and I've been selling him tickets for almost twenty years. What do you make of him?'

'I dunno,' Alf replied. 'Seems like a proper gentleman to me. Look how he's dressed. Nobody wears clothes like that nowadays; black jacket, striped pants, bowler hat, rolled umbrella and briefcase.'

'Yeah, I've heard he's retired long since,' Harry replied, 'but still goes to the city one day every month. I wish I had a good-paying job where I only had to work a few hours.'

'Somebody told me he's a bigwig in the financial district,' Alf said. 'An advisor to the government or something.'

'Oh, I can add to that,' Harry quickly replied. 'I met a chap last year who came into our pub and we somehow got to talking about some of our regular passengers. When I described George, he said he knew all about him. 'He's the person responsible for advising the government when a new budget is being prepared. A genius with figures. A local Einstein,' he said. 'I lied and told him you and I had already figured that out.'

George looked for his usual seat in the second carriage from the front, facing forwards. He hated traveling with his back to the engine. He liked to see where he was going, to look out of the window and enjoy the countryside. Having found his place, he carefully laid down the Financial Times on the seat next to him with the headlines clearly visible. Then, opening the London Times he smiled and snickered quietly as he read, his glasses almost touching the page. But he never failed to notice the inquisitive and furtive glances of the other passengers.

'I can't believe what's happening to this country,' a friendly voice chirped. 'Brexit, more bloody likely,

Brexshit to me. It's getting to the point where I might have to give up smoking. It's becoming just too damned expensive. We should never have left Europe. Give it a few more months and we probably won't be able to buy a bottle of French wine, or if it's available, will cost an arm and a leg. Got your ticket George?' A smiling ticket collector, held out his hand in anticipation.

'Well, good morning to you too, Syd,' George beamed. 'You're in fine fettle.'

'I would be if I was as close to the source as you are,' he said looking down at the Financial Times. 'You must be making a fortune with your investments. Couldn't you just give me one small tip. But no,' he said holding up his hand, 'I know it's illegal, insider information and all that. Just pretend you never heard me mention it.' He looked quickly around at the other passengers. But all seemed to be engrossed in their newspapers or on their cell phones. 'I guess I'll just have to go on dreaming or get on that TV show. What's it called, How To Become a Millionaire?'

'I'm sure you've got millions salted away already,' George joked. 'Aren't you intending to buy a house in the south of Spain?'

'Well, that's the dream plan,' he said wistfully. 'But I just wish that earlier in life I had entered a profession like yours. You're so damned lucky. And now a part-time job, once a month and just for a few hours. You're a lucky sod. And I'm sure your wife can afford anything she wants too. Not like my missus. Works three days a week as a care giver at the old folks' home so she can earn some money to play bingo every Tuesday and Friday, and enjoy a weekend boozing with her girlfriends.'

Handing back his ticket, Syd continued, 'Same time, same train next month, George and I'll still be here.' And with that, he moved on with checking tickets.

As the train pulled into Victoria Station, George gathered up his briefcase, papers and umbrella and joined the crowds heading for the exits. His next stop was across the road to the confectionery shop. Aldermans had been selling sweets of all kinds since the time of Charles Dickens, but for the past many years it was owned by the Turnbull family who had kept the trade name. George's purchases never varied; two Mars bars, a box of Cadbury's milk chocolates and a box of Pontefract Cakes.

'So nice to see you again, George.' A rather rotund, curly, grey-haired woman, probably in her early sixties, gave him a disarming smile. 'It's amazing how time flies. I can't imagine it's been a month already. How long has it been now? Must be almost twenty years we've known each other.'

'Actually, twenty-three,' George replied.

'Oh, yes, I remember now,' she said. 'That was after you got the promotion. You tried not to show it, but I could tell you were very happy. And look at you now, only having to work one day a month. The government must be very lucky to have you. I'm sure you could fully retire if you wanted to.'

'You are too kind, Mabel. And what about you? Aren't you getting ready for retirement?'

'Oh, Mr. George. I wish. But you know my William has been unable to work for so long. We have to make do with what I make here at the shop, which, thank God, continues to give us a living. His disability cheque hardly pays the rent. But I'm afraid of this Brexit thing. It will slow down the number of tourists coming into the city, and I rely so much on them. Not everybody is a regular customer like you. I'm so grateful for your business. You are so fortunate to work for the Bank of England. I'm sure you're well paid and no doubt your wife has everything she wants.'

George ignored the last remarks, a skill he had developed over the years. 'Well, I'm sure every little helps,' he replied, placing his purchases in his briefcase. 'Do take care, Mabel, and I'll see you next month.' He returned to the station and took the escalator down to the underground. As if on auto pilot, he followed the overhead direction panels to the Blue line that would take him on a fifty-minute journey to Walthamstow. It was always a crowded line, and difficult to find a seat until it had passed Kings Cross, which took about twenty minutes. The whole journey lasted almost an hour.

From Walthamstow, George took a cab and as it swung into a long, familiar tree-lined driveway, a huge red brick building rather like an English stately home, surrounded by trimmed lawns and well laid out flower beds, came into view. A sign at the entrance read, St. Anselm's Residential Home.

'How nice to see you again, Mr. Hatfield.' A pleasant looking and smiling woman looked down at him from the open doorway. 'Your sister has been eagerly waiting for you all morning. She will be so happy to see you.'

'And you too, Mrs. Williams. I trust you are well.'

'Well enough, indeed, sir, in spite of a little arthritis in the knee. But let me escort you through. You know the routine.'

Indeed, he knew it well. George understood that going through the metal detector was mainly for his own security, and once inside the locked door, was always surprised by the serenity and cleanliness of everything. Soft music played through a public address system. The décor was modern and in pastel colours, staff wore civilian clothing and there were plants and flowers everywhere. Mrs. Williams led George to a huge glass-covered sun lounge, where a couple of small groups were engaged in conversation. Her face lit up the moment he entered, and she rushed towards him, holding him in a tight hug. A slightly built, woman, wearing a brightly patterned dress, her grey hair pulled back and tied in a bun, Alice was three years younger than George. He stood there for a moment holding her, then gently eased her arms away and kissed the top of her head. Leading her by the hand to a small card table they sat opposite each other. Her care giver, Sandra, a wonderfully sensitive and capable young woman from Trinidad, withdrew to a discrete distance. That was the signal for Alice to take hold of George's briefcase. The routine never changed.

She took it and momentarily held it with both hands, looking at George expectantly, then placed it next to her. She knew precisely what would happen next. Taking the two newspapers from his coat pocket, he handed them to her. In a lightning move, she picked up the Financial Times, turned to the crossword puzzle, took a pencil off the table and waited. Alice giggled. George took out a pocket watch from his waistcoat and holding it in his hand, said 'Go.' The woman never looked up and only once seemed to hesitate, pausing for a moment as she chewed the end of her pencil. Then it was over. She laid the pencil down and looked at George. She heard him press the stop button.

'Four minutes and fifty-seven seconds, Alice,' he said.

'Thank you,' she replied in a sort of distant voice, but her eyes never left him.

Picking up the London Times, he waited until she had found the correct page, looked at his watch and then at her as she raised her pencil.

'Go,' he said.

These were their games. He couldn't remember exactly when they started, it was so long ago. But he did recall it was after the doctor informed him that his sister suffered from autism and was a savant. She could do complex mathematical equations in a fraction of the time it would take the average person, and they also discovered she was a genius at solving puzzles. In addition she had a photographic memory for words, yet she rarely spoke, lacked basic social skills and lived by routines. If ever they were broken or changed, it caused severe mental stress. But Alice also suffered from excessive mood swings and needed regular medication. George learned she was not capable of living on her own and needed twenty-four-hour care. St. Anselm's was the perfect place for her, and she seemed to be very happy there.

With a click, he stopped the watch. 'My goodness,' he exclaimed, 'you are getting faster each time I come. That was exactly five minutes and twelve seconds. You deserve a nice reward. Will you please open my briefcase and see what's inside?'

'Goodies,' she cried as she momentarily fumbled with the clasp then took out the two Mars bars, the Cadbury chocolates and the Pontefract cakes. There was no need to ask what she would eat first. Sandra came over and watched as Alice set aside one Mars bar, then took out four chocolates, one from each corner of the box and placed them in a line on the table. Next, she carefully tore the cellophane wrapper and extracted four Pontefract cakes setting them on top of the chocolates.

'Here is a paper bag I brought for you,' Sandra said softly. 'Why not put them inside and enjoy them throughout the day? I will hold the rest for you. You know I will help you ration them. You can enjoy them every evening when you watch the Wheel of Fortune.'

'Yes, goodies tomorrow and next tomorrow,' Alice cried, 'That's two full days, forty-eight hours, one hundred and seventy-two thousand, eight hundred seconds.'

Other than the seasons and the weather, the meeting never changed. For George, this was the way it had been for more than twenty years.

As he rode the train back to Crawley, and the regular passengers nodded at him, he realized that nobody in the whole world knew who he really was, and smiled inwardly. For more than thirty years, he had worked as a janitor at the London Stock Exchange. As his eyesight, that had always been poor, deteriorated, he went out on disability. That was his sole source of income. He wasn't married, didn't smoke or drink and lived frugally in a one-room apartment in a converted large Victorian house. He had one pastime; he was writing a novel about a man who wanted to be a stockbroker.

'A good day at the office, then?' Alf asked

solicitously as he walked out of the station to take the bus home.

'Never, better,' George replied with a smile on his face and spring in his step. 'Never, better.'

# MAY

# Clemency

## Rob Molan

*chamomile tea*

Coming out of the warmth of the café into the cold is always a shock at this time of year and my fingers start to freeze as I'm locking up. I notice the homeless guy is lying in the doorway of the empty shop next door again. He's wrapped up in a blue sleeping bag and resting on a cardboard mattress with his head covered with a balaclava. Mary from the bread shop was complaining about him when she was in this morning but I feel sorry for the poor sod. I remember my social worker pal telling me that many rough sleepers have been in prison, the army or care and struggle to lead independent lives after entering the outside world.

I'm running late. I told Kay I would meet her in the pub at eight and it's twenty past. There's so much I need to do now before I can get away at night. I look for a taxi but the first few aren't free. I'm shivering with the cold and regret not putting on my extra thick, woolly tights. Eventually, a free cab appears which whisks me off to Camden Town.

The pub is packed and I see Kay sitting at a table with a big frown on her face and an empty glass in front of her, and rush over.

'I'm so sorry I'm late.'

'Thank God you're here, Brigid. I've had some creep hitting on me. I called but you didn't pick up.' She's got new highlights in her hair.

I look inside my handbag.

'Damn. I've left my mobile in the café and will have to go back later. But let me get some drinks.'

Once we have two large glasses of Malbec on the table we start chatting.

'So how are you?' asks Kay resting her chin on a hand. 'I've not seen you for ages.'

'Cream crackered. Having your lover as a business partner is great when things are going well but not so when you break up and you're left to run things yourself. Tim didn't pull his weight. There was always a reason why he had to nip out during the day or finish early, leaving muggins here on her own. Whenever I complained, he was apologetic but nothing changed and I finally snapped one day and gave him his marching orders. He pleaded with me but wasn't getting another chance.'

'I'm sorry to hear that. But I heard you had a young woman helping you.'

'I had to let her go a couple of weeks ago. She missed a few shifts due to childcare problems and I couldn't rely on her.'

I take a sip of wine.

'She was upset when I told her the news complaining that Christmas was coming up but she had blown the opportunity I'd given her. I've advertised for a replacement but have had no luck so far. Brexit has made it much harder to recruit staff in the sector.'

Kay frowns. I need to change the subject.

'Sorry, that's enough of me moaning. When did you change your hairstyle? It suits you.'

'I'm glad you like it. I had it done last week.' She smiles patting her head.

Our conversation then takes off in all sorts of directions, including holiday plans for our forthcoming birthdays – we're both about to hit forty. Time flies and when I realise it's nearly ten thirty. I make my excuses and leave, and jump on a bus back to King's Cross. I get off at the stop opposite the café and spot a commotion outside the shop next door. Crossing the road, I see three young men kicking the homeless guy on the ground and him wrapped up into a ball to protect himself. I run over and shout at them.

'Hey, stop that. I'm calling the police.' I may be petite but I've got a powerful pair of lungs.

They turn around and then look at each other before scarpering. I know I took a risk there but the adrenalin kicked in.

'I'll get help,' I say to the poor bloke who is writhing in pain and moaning.

I let myself into the café and call 999 and ask for the police and an ambulance before returning outside. I bend down and the street light reveals streaks of blood running down his greyish skin into a matted beard.

'They won't be long. I said you needed urgent assistance.' His eyes are closed but thankfully he's still breathing.

The ambulance arrives ten minutes later and the police shortly afterwards.

'Did you get a clear view of the men?' a young officer asks.

'No. They had their hoods up and only turned round briefly. I hope you catch the thugs.'

The paramedics attend to the victim, carefully place him on a stretcher and carry him into the back of the ambulance. As it disappears into the night, a sense of exhaustion overwhelms me as I start the trek home back to my flat along the frosty pavement.

I'm pulling my hair out here. I've got four orders for a full English and other customers waiting for takeaway bacon rolls who are getting impatient. And the flaming coffee machine is playing up again.

I hear the door open and, in the corner of my eye, see a tall chap enter and approach the counter.

'I'll be with you shortly,' I say.

'No problem, Brigid. Take your time.' I turn and find his bright blue eyes staring at me.

I don't recognise him. He's clean shaven and has cropped blonde hair and a long thin jaw.

'It's me, the homeless guy you rescued,' he says

softly. 'You might not recognise me as I was in a right state the last time you saw me.'

'Oh, it's great to see you looking so well.' He's younger than I thought, probably in his mid-thirties.

'Grab a seat and I'll be with you as soon as I can.'

He nods and walks over to a table by the window.

When the rush is over, I make two instant coffees, take them over and sit down beside him.

'So how are you?'

'I'm fine now. The bruising on my ribs is a lot better and the headaches have stopped. I was released from hospital two weeks ago and have moved into a hostel. If you hadn't had the guts to chase off those lads, God knows where I would be now. I'm ever so grateful.'

'I had to do something. Have they caught the bastards?'

'Not to my knowledge.' He shrugs his shoulders.

'What are your plans?'

'I've signed on and am looking for a job. I want to stand on my own feet.'

I don't often have light bulb moments but this is one of them.

'If you're interested, I can let you have a few hours a day here. It will just be washing dishes, clearing and wiping tables and it will be cash in hand.'

'Brilliant. When can I start?' He jumps up.

'Be here at seven thirty tomorrow. What's your name by the way?'

‘Keith. The policeman who took my statement was kind enough to tell me yours.’

‘Welcome on board, Keith.’

‘How does Moses brew his coffee?’

‘No idea.’

‘Hebrews it!’

‘Groan!’ Keith keeps coming out with these corny jokes. ‘Can you pop up that bread in the toaster before it turns into a cinder?’

‘No problem,’ he replies.

I’ve had a smile on my face at work since he started six weeks ago. More importantly, he’s a real grafter, washing and scrubbing anything and everything, leaving the tables spotless after clearing them. And the coffee machine is never out of action now. He’s also showing an interest in helping me with the cooking.

The customers love him. A few taxi drivers were sitting round a table the other day and Keith was loading dirty dishes onto a tray.

‘Don’t you get fed up with Brigid bossing you about?’ asked one of them with a twinkle in his eye.

‘No, I’ve had worse. You know I was in a cab yesterday and the driver said he loved his job as nobody told him what to do. He wasn’t happy though when I told him to turn left.’

‘You should be on the stage. Then I could heckle you,’ laughs another.

When grumpy Mary came in and met Keith for the first time, she started flirting with him.

'So where did you appear from?' she asked in a husky voice.

'I was hiding in plain sight,' he replied with a big grin.

She looked at him blankly and I couldn't stop myself giggling.

It's also handy to have him around when customers kick off, like one did last week.

'I gave you a twenty, love, but you've given me change from a ten.' The big lump was sticking his hand out as he eyeballed me.

'No. It was definitely a tenner,' I replied calmly.

'I'll come round the other side and take what you owe me,' he threatened, jabbing a finger at me.

Keith was across in a flash and pulled himself up to his full height.

'That wouldn't be very clever, sir. Would it?' The oaf turned and sloped off without replying.

Today, I need a favour from Keith.

'Can you stay a bit later tonight and cash up for me?' I've shown him how to do this and trust him with the till. 'I need to get away an hour early so I can complete my tax return. While I'm at it, I'll register you for tax and national insurance contributions. It's time to put you on the books.'

'That's great. I've got my benefit slip in my jacket in a minute and it's got my national insurance number on it.'

Later at home, I spend several hours working on the return. When it's finally submitted, I take Keith's benefit slip out of my handbag before logging onto the registration website. Funnily, I've never asked him what his surname is and when I see it in black and white my stomach lurches.

I never saw the robber's face when he grabbed the handbag off my shoulder and sprinted away. I was summoned though a few months later to give evidence in the trial of a certain Keith Coady. But the case never went to trial in the end because he was charged with a string of other, similar offences and changed his plea to guilty to all of them. That was four years ago but I still remember the shock of being robbed by a stranger and the feelings of anxiety when I went out on my own in the weeks which followed.

I don't like being taken for a mug and will have it out with him tomorrow. But I need to get to bed now as I can't keep my eyes open.

'Good morning, Brigid. How are you?' Now he has his own key, he's usually in before me.

I don't reply and walk through to the back and hang up my coat. I take a deep breath before coming back to the front.

'Err, I've made a brew for us.' He looks sideways at me.

I take the mug from him, have a sip of the hot, sweet coffee and look him in the eye.

'When did you get out of prison?'

His face goes beetroot.

'Is it that obvious I was inside?'

'Let's call it an educated guess.'

His shoulders slump.

'Six months ago.' His voice drops. 'I didn't want to go back to the life and people I knew before and so ended up living on the streets. I was hoping to find a job and somewhere to live but had almost given up by the time I got beaten up by those guys. Surviving that gave me renewed hope and then you gave me this chance.'

'It would have been better if you'd told me this before. Don't you think?'

'Yes,' he mumbles.

'I'd be within my rights to sack you.'

He nods slowly and starts to take off his apron.

'But I'm not going to.'

His jaw slackens.

'I've booked a city break with a friend next week to celebrate our birthdays and I need you to manage the café while I'm away. And when I get back, I'm going to increase your hours.'

Maybe I'm turning soft but I've had enough of working twelve hour days and anyway the guy has earned himself a break.

'You won't regret it. I promise you.'

'I'd better not, otherwise you'll be back sleeping in doorways. Anyway, we need to get a move on, we're opening in a few minutes.'

# Three Little Words

## Claire Jaggard

### *fizzy pop*

What the girl staring at Joey needed right now was a people person.

It was just her luck that Joey was more comfortable with numbers.

His last form teacher, Mrs Jefferies, had been a people person. She'd valued a firm handshake and a steady gaze. Joey's slouchy lollop and downcast eyes had dismayed her and, regretfully, she'd pencilled 'NP' beside his name in the register: 'No Potential'. The fact that Joey could tot up lunch money faster than any of his classmates or remember the combination to the lock on the stationery cupboard every time she forgot it counted for nothing to Mrs Jefferies.

Starved of encouragement to look beyond the end of his nose, Joey had settled for a job at the only petrol station in town. He hadn't even applied for the role, more fallen into it by accident when Mr Healey the owner lost his temper one afternoon and sacked the previous incumbent. Joey had been sitting on the forecourt cooling off with a can of drink, and mumbled that he could help out, maybe, until Mr Healey found someone better.

The quiet late shifts were the ones Joey preferred. Few customers called by after nightfall, and those who did rarely wanted to make small talk. As long as he offered the appropriate grunts and the correct change, Joey could keep one ear plugged into the radio as he worked, and the hours simply slipped by.

Out of habit, he memorised number plates, gradually stacking the local regulars into his mental filing cabinet. The blue van that had just pulled up wasn't one he recognised. Must be an out of towner.

The driver opened the back of the van to let out a passenger, but that didn't strike Joey as unusual. A new radio host had taken over his favourite show, and Joey was still in two minds about the cheeky chappie presentation style. The girl half fell out of the van and the man gripped her arm as she recovered her balance.

That left him with just one hand to fumble the petrol flap open and fill the van, but Joey couldn't leave his post to offer help. Mr Healey had impressed this on him time and again. Joey had easily committed the van's number plate to memory by the time the driver banged the dispenser back onto the pump.

Inside the shop, the man steered the girl towards the customer toilet and hovered nearby, fingers drumming against denim-clad thighs until she slid out again.

Joey's own standards of personal grooming had stopped Mrs Jefferies in her tracks on more than one occasion, but even he could see this girl was a mess. Greasy hair lay plastered against her forehead, her clothes hung too loosely and her eyes were red and swollen.

Her eyes. They'd locked onto his the minute she'd emerged from the toilet, and stayed there. Her mouth opened and shut, but she said nothing. Joey felt himself redden and broke the connection, looking down at the till.

The man grabbed crisps, sweets and a large bottle of fizzy drink and dumped them on the counter, pulling out his wallet while Joey carefully scanned each item.

'That's twenty one fifty seven, please.'

Joey started to pack the snacks into a carrier bag, but the bottle toppled over and the girl reached out to catch it on a reflex. Their hands met awkwardly, his warmth transferring to her cold fingers, her eyes still boring into his. Joey disentangled himself and righted the bottle, but not before the man lost patience.

He tossed down two grubby twenty pound notes, snatched the bag with one hand and the girl with the other, and turned to leave.

'Keep the change.'

Three little words.

'But that's…'

Joey's brain sputtered, and for once, failed to compute.

'… too much.'

No-one tips petrol station cashiers, and no-one walks away from the best part of twenty quid.

They were already at the door, the man's hand pushing firmly into the small of the girl's back. She threw Joey one last beseeching look before sagging out towards the van.

Joey shrugged, screwed up the receipt and tossed it into the bin. He turned his attention back to the radio. It was the top of the hour, and the news jingle ushered in a calmer voice. The lead story was still that girl who'd disappeared a few days ago. No-one had yet given the police any useful information, despite a handsome reward on offer.

The stories faded in importance and the newsreader wrapped up with a cheery anecdote. Joey pulled out his ear plugs. The petrol station was empty now, quiet save for the soothing background hum of lights and coolers.

Joey wondered idly how he would spend a reward that generous.

He eyed the folded notes still lying on the counter.

'Keep the change,' the man had said.

Should he though? Something didn't add up. Joey sat for a long while reviewing the situation, his brain tumbling and fumbling towards an explanation that he didn't like, but couldn't dismiss.

Slowly, very slowly, Joey's hand reached for the phone.

# JUNE

# The Train to London

## Henry Lewi

### *bottled water*

He settled into his seat on the London bound train well ahead of its departure. It had been a fun month playing the clubs around Manchester and the North of England; he'd played as a solo musician, played alongside other jazz and blues groups, and most recently had joined up with a Folk-punk group for the last four days of his stay in Manchester.

He always liked to board his train early, choose his seat, always a window, and always at a table, always facing front; he placed his two old battered leather suitcases on the rack above and settled into his seat.

There were no delays, the train was going to leave on time and the journey would take just under three hours to Euston. He'd occupy the time reading the latest best-selling thriller he'd bought at the station bookshop. Much better than driving, or being parked for hours on the M6 and M1.

The carriage began to fill up: a few businessmen, couples, and across the aisle, the four members of the Folk-punk group he'd recently played alongside. Despite their appearance, long hair, heavily mascaraed eyes, T-shirts and leather jackets, he knew that all four were postgraduate students, currently completing their

PhDs in mathematics, biochemistry and astrophysics. Bright lads, but they would probably make more money in their music than they'd ever do following their graduation.

Two older ladies occupied the two outer seats at his table and an overweight, red-faced young man forced his way into the remaining window seat opposite, and placed his laptop on the table between them. He hung his jacket on the hook alongside his seat, his red braces stretched taught over his striped shirt and belly.

The train pulled out of Manchester on time, and began its journey on to London, the steady passage of the train lulling him to sleep whilst he struggled to read his book. He was woken by the man opposite talking loudly into his phone, with the speaker on, and a lengthy loud conversation ensuing, which involved a lot of swearing, yelling, and discussions on how much money the so-called businessman was going to make.

Suddenly the woman seated next to him said to the fat businessman, 'I'm sorry, could you be a little less loud, maybe turn off your phone and be a little bit more considerate, and possibly tone down your language?'

'Shut up Granny,' he replied. 'This is my business, my job, so don't interfere,' and continued to shout into his phone whilst looking at his laptop.

The train continued on its journey, clickety-clack,

clickety-clack; there was still over two hours to go to London. The woman looked as if she was about to burst into tears and looked away; he looked at the fat businessman in his red braces, holding his phone in one hand and tapping away on his laptop.

'Did you really have to be that rude?' he asked.

'What's it to you? replied the businessman, 'I'm making more money than the lot of you, so zip it OK?' as he continued to speak loudly on the phone.

'Your final word?' he asked.

'Yes it's my fucking final word,' replied the businessman.

With that he stood up in his seat and brought down the smaller of his two battered cases and opening it took out his trumpet. Taking a swig of water from his ever-present water bottle, he moistened his lips, put the trumpet to his mouth.

He blew a couple of notes and began to play the *Mexican Hat Dance*. '♪♪*da-da-da*♪ – ♪*da da- dada*♪♪,' he played whilst the carriage went quiet.

The fat businessman shouted at him, 'Oi! Can it, I'm trying to work here.'

'So am I, so am I,' replied the trumpeter quietly. 'You do your job and I'll do mine,' and immediately launched into a trumpet solo version of *When the Saints Go Marching In*. As he played on, people in the carriage began to sing along, so he continued, and next played *All you need is Love*, by which time the whole carriage joined in and were singing the words.

The four members of the Folk-punk group had by now retrieved their instruments, two banjos, a mandolin and acoustic guitar, and took over, playing their own versions of Vivaldi's mandolin and guitar concertos, with him jamming along with them on his trumpet, as the carriage now rocked, cheered and videoed the performance. The music continued as people from other carriages squeezed in, watching, cheering and clapping along to the music, even the train conductors came along to observe and applaud.

Unable to hear himself think, let alone continue with his phone call, the fat businessman, got up and forced his way out of the carriage to loud jeers; but still the music played on, the passengers listened, and applauded as the impromptu concert continued, as they all travelled en-route to London.

By the time the train had pulled into Euston, the YouTube video that had been posted and had been viewed well over a million times, and that night the local news reports were showing video clips from the train journey, with one critic stating that the spontaneous performers had 'played their instruments like Heavenly Angels'.

The news that night was also reporting that the police had arrested a businessman arriving on the same train for fraud and embezzlement, and he'd stand trial later that month.

As he watched the YouTube video clips of himself playing with the Folk-punk group on the news that night, the Archangel Gideon, spread his wings wide with satisfaction and played one last song on his Heavenly Trumpet.

# My Weekend at Grammy's

Laura Sukonick

***an old fashioned made with bourbon, no garnishes***

'I'm here,' I called as I walked my 8 year old self through my grandparents' never-locked backdoor. I waved goodbye to my parents as they backed their car out of the long driveway. With their only child officially under her grandmother's care, their weekly date night with each other had begun at 4pm. So had my weekly date night; with my grandmother.

'HERE I come,' was the instant response to my greeting from my grandmother's disembodied voice. My grandmother didn't have the winey, nasal tone that sitcom viewers are used to hearing in their Jewish American moms. Instead, she sounded like a prepubescent Louis Armstrong who was immersed in a closing statement in court. Her voice was gruff, but still shrill, and never without total certainty.

She pre-punctuated her important sentences with a fast inhale. During this inhale she would open and close her bright pinked lips several times like she was revving up her jaw before speaking. After about five revs of the jaw she'd floor it into a story at 70 miles/ hour.

'Where are you?' I called, Marco-Polo-ing my way around the perimeter of her first floor.

'I'm on the tor-let,' she called back. She always

added Rs to words that don't have Rs. I made my way down the hall to the powder room that Grandmom was yelling at me from. Taped to the shut bathroom door was a sheet of yellow legal pad paper with 'TOILET BROKEN!' scribbled in blue ink.

'What's wrong with your toilet?' I called to the other side of the door.

'Nothing's wrong with it.'

'Then what's with the sign?'

'I put it there so no one uses it,' she responded with casual satisfaction as the toilet flushed.

Ten seconds later the bathroom door flung open. Framed in the doorway was Grandmom in a loose floor-length skirt, still drying her hands with a towel. Upon seeing me she gasped with excitement and threw her head back so that her open mouth was facing the ceiling. With the drying towel still in her hand she propelled herself out of the bathroom doorway. Once in the hallway she began slapping her thighs in delight. (The left thigh she slapped with her palm facing upwards. The right thigh she slapped with the towel.) Next she proceeded to shout Yiddish terms of endearment, slapping her thighs all the while to keep time. Like a spiritual, Yiddish, drill sergeant. Instead of 'MARCH MARCH. MARCH MARCH,' she was shouting, 'SHAY-NA. PUH-NUM.'

Finally, she embraced me in an aggressively tight hug. Clinging to me, and the towel, she shifted her weight back and forth from her left foot to her right foot. With each sway she let out a guttural 'OY!' This greeting ritual, which she performed on a weekly basis, was her demonstration of love that is so intense that it's literally uncontainable.

'NU?' Grandmom asked me as we headed upstairs. She then immediately translated that to, 'What's doing with you?' As always I was eager to answer. I knew from experience that she would wholeheartedly celebrate anything I was currently excited about. That day I was giving her a run for her money.

For some reason that is beyond comprehension, the new cool trend at my suburban elementary school happened to be collecting magazine advertisements featuring Absolut Vodka bottles. The coolest kids even had them in plastic sleeves, which they kept organized in three-ring binders. I loved the idea of having something to collect, organize and trade with the other kids. The absurdity of what that item was did not occur to me.

When Grandmom caught wind that I'd become deeply invested in collecting trash advertising liquor, at the age of eight, she laughed, shook her head, and then jumped into action. Together we rummaged through the huge stacks of Times Magazines that my grandfather hoarded by the dozens on his unusable desk. We even emptied the trash cans just in case the AARP was advertising my unlikely new favourite product. By dinner time I had myself a collection of

Vodka ads large enough to garner the admiration of the entire fourth grade. We were over the moon about it.

We celebrated over our usual weekend dinner together: buttered noodles and caffeine free diet coke, with baked apples for dessert.

'The food is GROWing on your plate, not shrinking,' she expressed to me with concern. This meant I wasn't eating quickly enough to assure her that I was satisfied with the food. (To be fair, no one ever did anything quickly enough for her – the woman took a vacation like she was getting it over with, and expected everybody to follow suit.)

'You don't like it,' she worried. 'I'll make something else.'

'It's good! I'm eating,' I reassured her honestly with my mouth full. I knew I could've told her if I didn't want it. My reassurance did not appease her.

'Eating?! You took one bite and looked ill. Now you're turning green on me, like the wicked witch in Oz.' Grandmom liked to insert a movie reference into her statement when she felt she was making a strong point.

'Don't forget your coat,' she'd exasperatedly remind me each Sunday when Mom and Dad came to pick me up, 'because come tomorrow it'll be Gone With the Wind in the dump!' Her repertoire was mostly Hollywood classics from the 1930s.

Before long the phone rang.

'CHRIST ALMIGHTY,' my grandfather screamed from his horizontal EZ chair in the living room, making himself known for the first of two times that evening. Grandpop always shouted curses when a noise was louder than he preferred it to be.

'Lauralah is here so DO NOT YELL,' she screamed immediately back.

'WHO?'

*ring*

'CHRIST!!'

'LAURA.'

'Laura's here?'

'JESUS CHRIST!'

'Let it go,' Grandmom instructed me as usual. (Meaning the phone, to voicemail.) But when the person leaving the voicemail turned out to be her brother, he barely got one word out before she lunged for the phone.

'What's wrong, Norm?!' he shouted into the receiver that was still traveling to her mouth. Nothing was wrong. He called every day. She consistently greeted him this way.

Norm was Grandmom's best friend and older brother. He was her only sibling. He was older; she was tougher. They grew up looking out for each other while their family endured antisemitism and poverty. Until the day she died she talked to him like she might have to drop everything and physically defend him at any moment.

The conversation then proceeded as it always did: 'Did you eat, Norm?' 'What'd you eat?' Pause. 'Was it fresh?' Then the indiscriminate grumbling of uncle Norm became audible from the phone speaker, to which, every minute or so, Grandmom would respond with another 'Absolutely'. She pronounced it like 'aha-bsolutely'. This proceeded for about ten minutes until the inevitable, 'Okay Norm. Gay Gezunt, Norm. Call me if you need anything.' And then one more, 'Gay Gezunt, Norm. Bye.'

After dinner and baked apples, I dressed myself in one of Grandmom's old fur coats as Grandmom summoned my grandfather at my request.

'HERBERT,' she yelled to him from the hallway. 'Herbert, Laura wants to sing for us in the living room. Come here.'

'Again?!' He had a point. This was a weekly occurrence.

'Herbert,' she warned him coldly, 'DO not start.'

Dutifully my grandfather began the four minute process of getting himself out of his EZ chair. He narrated his annoyance about the ordeal as he moved. Once he arrived in the shag carpeted living room, he began the four minute process of noisily sitting himself down on the sofa.

When I was satisfied that my two audience members were accounted for, I explained that I would first be singing Hey Big Spender. I had recently become aware of this sensual tune because my cousin had learned it in her dance class and then taught it to me. I began swaying my hips and singing terribly while draped in Grandmom's enormous fox coat. As if on cue my grandfather immediately fell asleep.

I finished my first song to a standing ovation from Grandmom.

I then announced, 'Intermission.' This was so I could feel like a sophisticated cocktail waitress while I scooped a diet coke can out of the refrigerator for my grandmother, and handed it to her in exchange for her dollar. She loved the gimmick and tipped me for my trouble.

'Intermission is over,' I announced. At this point my grandfather had an announcement of his own.

'That's all for me, Sweetheart,' he said in an exhale, already on the crawl back to his horizontal chair in the living room. He would remain there until the following morning.

After the show Grandmom and I played pickup sticks and Rummy500 (the latter of which she had just taught me the week before). Then it was time to get ready for bed.

Inside her shower I found the usual supplies: a bar of dove soap, a bottle of Pert Plus shampoo, and an absolutely massive unbranded jar, with a screw top lid, of the thickest, most effective hair conditioner I have ever used to this day. I have no idea what it was.

'Leave your bloomers off, hon,' Grandmom

called to me as I was putting on my pyjamas in the bathroom. 'Bloomers' is what she called underwear.

'I know, Grandmom.'

'You need to air out your knish overnight,' she espoused. 'It's healthy!'

With that we turned on the Golden Girls and climbed in bed. After Golden Girls ended she went downstairs and re-emerged with two unpeeled oranges in her hand.

'Here Dolly.'

I took one of the oranges knowing exactly what to do. I slid it under my left armpit and then snuggled myself under the blankets.

'Did you really used to do this with your grandmother?' I asked her.

'Aha-bsolutely,' she confirmed, slipping her own orange under her own left armpit.

'We'll eat them in the morning and it'll bring good luck. You'll see.'

Five minutes later she was snoring loudly. When I touched her arm gently her body instantly jerked upright while she shouted, 'I'M AWAKE WHAT'S WRONG?!'

'Grandmom,' I whispered, unfazed. I was used to her waking up in an explosion.

'Huh mummulah?'

'Can you tell me a story?'

'Okay honey.'

'About Arlo the horse.'

'Okay, let me think of something.'

'Okay.'

I waited. And waited. And then suddenly she was snoring again.

I could smell the Tropicana orange in my armpit as the familiar clank of her rattling pipes began to fill the room.

'It's OK,' I whispered between her snores. With my two small hands, I softly guided her head back down to the pillow before whispering, 'You can tell me the story next week.'

# Echoes

## Peter Lingard

***a pint of best bitter***

For a fraction of a second, I see her smile, but it passes so quickly I cannot be sure if it was a trick of my imagination or an actual memory. I am not even sure if I saw the smile in her eyes or on her lips.

I remember more of Anne, the farmer's daughter who smelled of soap. Her hazel eyes sparkled when she smiled. Her large frame, muscled torso and short, curly hair come easily to mind. I swapped Anne for Frances, an accountant's daughter who smelled of perfume. Why is it I can recall Anne with relative ease, but only have smoky, wispy glimpses of Frances? Did I make a mistake? Is my memory telling me I should have stayed with Anne?

If I *had* stuck with Anne, would she and I still be together? What of the women who have loved me since then? Their influences have helped forge the man I am. If Anne had been my last and enduring love, I would be a different me. I would probably like myself more, but I would miss all the fabulous females who have filled my life since then.

Anne liked to carry my kit to rugby games. My older girlfriend and status symbol cleaned my boots after every game and rubbed dubbing into the leather. Not trusting my mother to do a good enough job, she washed and ironed my strip. (I felt uncomfortable when teammates grinned at my clean strip with creases down the shirtsleeves and the front of my shorts. I threw the items on the floor of the changing room to scruff them with my feet and Anne occasionally asked why my strip looked dirty before the game started.) We travelled by public transport to the stadium, my kit securely held by Anne. She always gave me a good-luck kiss on my cheek before tucking her hair beneath the edges of her scarf and taking her cold and lonely seat in the empty stands, waiting an hour or more for the game to begin. Sometimes, she embarrassed me by vocalising her less than knowledgeable encouragement during the game.

In the club bar afterwards, she stayed constantly by my side, leaving only to purchase more beer for her underage boyfriend or to attempt to convince the cub reporter from the local newspaper that my name should be included in his summary. When older teammates tried to impress Anne by telling her age equalled experience, she told them she was true to me and they laughed. Whenever I received a lump or a scratch, her loving care embarrassed me.

I tried to change her and she tried to change me while Frances beckoned from the wings.

Schooling ranked high on Anne's priorities list. While she studied for summer exams, I put sugar in the petrol tank of the math teacher's car, ordered a ton of manure delivered to the English teacher's house on a c.o.d. basis, and sent a letter of resignation to the head master in the name of the physics teacher. For these acts, I was encouraged to abandon my scholastic endeavours. While Anne did her homework, I drank beer and hung out in the town's toughest bars. When the police arrested me for underage drinking, disturbing the peace and causing mayhem, Anne secured my release and made promises for me that I had no intention of keeping.

Good, kind Anne wore knee-length dresses, white blouses and sensible sweaters. Sultry Frances wore short shorts and revealing tops. I suppose it is telling that I can remember the shorts and tops, but not the person who filled them. When my friend, Allen Doyle told me he wanted to date Frances, I got there before him.

Sorry, Anne but you made me treat you so.

Frances *seemed* sophisticated, but her money went on cheap rooms in hotels where the proprietors never questioned what a pair of fifteen-year-olds was doing there. In those dark and dusty rooms where the curtains were forever closed, she taught me more about sex than a girl of her age should know.

# JULY

# Juniper

Monica Goertzen Hertlein

*pine needle tea*

I am alive.

My seed cracks and I stretch, up and down. Warm soil envelopes me, dark and moist. My tiny roots search for nourishment, for water, anchoring me to this place.

Above the dirt, the light is heavy. Thick. Stale. Rich soil feeds me, almost saccharine. I grow too fast but soak it up, anyway.

I am separated from my root-mates. New soil surrounds me, anchors me, still saccharine rich. I survived.

I grow, tall and straight. Adult greenery clothes me.

We are separated. Can I live this way, roots constrained, segregated from my nearby siblings?

Other, more distant, relations are here. Some are prickly. Some spread sideways or curl in round balls. Further away are more distant relations, fleeting but colourful, perfuming stale air.

At the faintest edge of my consciousness are kin whose relationship I barely sense. Fleeting, too, but in constant motion. They move among us, often in groups. Some bend near, to sniff or touch or offer sustenance.

'We'll take five.'

I am relocated again. I am disoriented, but conscious.

At last, I breathe air that lives and moves, air with a thousand new scents. And the light! It is full and sweet. I spread to catch as much as I can. And the soil is rich, not as heavy with nutrients but wider and bustling with life. My roots test their limits. They have none.

'Fills the spot nicely, don't you think?'

'Looks great, dear.'

A few siblings stand near me, lined up in the shade of a tall structure, beside an area thick with grass. Our branches caress each other.

Excited, yet content, I reach taller and taller still and dig deeper and deeper. I drink water and absorb the beautiful sunlight and breathe into the moving, scented air.

When the periods of sunlight dwindle, my blood slows, ready for an oncoming cold I have yet to experience. My siblings do the same. Nearby, our close relations show their true colours, no longer hidden beneath our shared green blood.

Water is more difficult to find, though frozen droplets coat my green foliage. The air is sharper, the many scents muted. The grass sleeps. Our ambulatory kin move swiftly if they venture out.

Between one breath and the next the stretches of daylight grow longer. Air and soil are thick with moisture, soaking my roots. The grass wakes. Our noble kin shed the last dried bits of brown, all that remains of their previous colours, and sprout leaves in a multitude of shapes.

We grow taller, reach deeper. By the time the trees change colours several times more, I can see over the roof of the structure that shades my siblings and me. There are many buildings, more than I guessed, spread out around me, interspersed with my tallest kin, stems thicker than all my siblings together. Some remain green the way we do, towering above rooftops, wider and pricklier than we but comforting in their nearness.

I become a haven for not just the tiniest of our mobile relations, who burrow in my bark or nibble my leaves, but some of those that soar on the perfumed, moving air. They perch on my branches and chatter to each other in sweet voices, even their arguments like songs.

Occasionally, a warm-blooded kin stealthily climbs my narrow limbs, attention focused on their feathery cousins. Our common relative, one of those busy kin who feeds me, watches, alternately amused and scolding.

Once again, the hours of sunlight lengthen. My roots are deep enough that the soil remains soft and warm but I relish the familiar dampness in spring dirt and air, sweet with moisture.

There is a loud noise, loud enough to vibrate on the fresh air. One of my siblings cries in pain. Two of our mobile relatives are near but they are not feeding us today.

The sound repeats in fits and starts. Our feathered cousins scatter. Our fur-coated relatives cower and hiss or run. Only our distant relations are unbothered, moving among us.

My nearest sibling trembles and cries. Our linked branches pull apart. I am surprised. Our kind stand for much longer than the breaths we have sent into the air.

Our mobile cousins move with purpose, removing my prone siblings, one after another. Then the noise is impossibly louder, vibrating through me. Agony.

I shudder. I fall.

I am prone on the grass which has barely woken from its most recent sleep. I no longer feel my roots. Sunlight touches my foliage as my breath fades.

I am moved again but my senses dim.

My green fades. Soon, I will be brown and stiff.

My final breaths exhale.

My roots shrivel. The soil above them is covered in bright white stones.

'Fills the spot nicely, don't you think?'

'Looks great, dear.'

# Simon Hope

## Jim Bates

### *Arnie Palmer*

My assistant, Jan Walkin, knocked on the door, took three steps across the floor, and dropped a sheet of paper on my desk. 'Here's the report, Simon.' She shrugged her thin shoulders. 'Such as it is.'

I turned to her from staring out the second-floor window of the office I rented. 'Such as it is?' I asked. 'That's a helluva thing to say.'

Jan puffed up to the full height of her four-foot-ten-inch frame and said, 'It's a helluva business you've got going here, Simon.' She pointed to the one book on the bookshelf behind my desk. 'Pretending to be like your hero.' It was my treasured collection of Sherlock Holmes.

'So... What's your point?' I asked.

'What's your favourite story?'

'*The Woman in Red.*'

'Conan Doyle's first full-length novel. Right?'

'Exactly. I love that one.'

'What else?'

'Well, there's *The Hound of the Baskervilles.*'

'Another novel.'

'Correct. And *The Adventure of the Dancing Men* and *A Scandal in Bohemia* and...'

'Right. Short Stories. And if I stood here all day, I'm sure you'd name them all.'

'Well…'

I flushed, embarrassed. She was right. I had loved Sherlock Holmes since I was twelve years old. Ever since my aunt had given me the *Complete Sherlock Holmes* shortly after I'd come to live with her after my parents had been killed in a car accident. My older brother and sister had died, too. I had been in the same accident and was in bad shape physically and emotionally, but I eventually recovered. Physically anyway. It's been a long time emotionally. Twenty-five years but who's counting? Ha, ha. Escaping with Sherlock has helped immensely.

'So what?' I said.

'I know you want to be a detective like him. I respect that.'

'Your point being?'

She nodded at the photos on the wall. Scotty, the Tennessee Walker, who I'd found in a stud farm in Iowa. Hector, the German Shepard guide dog I rescued from a breeding kennel north of Minneapolis in Chisago Country. Snowflake, a terminally ill boy's treasured kitten who had wandered off and been locked in a storage shed for a week. I'd found them all. It's what I did. I found lost pets.

'My point is that Sherlock used his smarts and intuition to solve crimes, find jewels, and stop wars from happening. You…' She pointed at my photos on the wall. In addition to the three I'd mentioned there were over a dozen more. 'You just…' She slammed her hand on my desk making me jump. 'Oh, I don't know. It just seems like you aren't trying hard enough.' She shook her head. 'Like you're just pretending to play detective rather than truly being one.' She pointed to my framed photo of Jeremy Brett as Sherlock on the corner of my desk. 'Mark my words, your hero Sherlock would just laugh his ass off.'

With that scathing comment, she turned on her heel and left. *Oh, yeah*, I said to myself. *Well, we'll see about that!* Not the pithiest retort, I'll grant you, but hell, I didn't want to piss her off any more than she already was. Once we'd been lovers. Now? Now I was lucky she was working with me.

Her words were harsh, and, compared to Sherlock Holmes and his abilities, probably true. But I couldn't help it. I liked my job. I liked animals. My best friend for years was my aunt's big tabby cat named Rusty.

I looked around my office. I liked my Persian rug and the false fireplace. I liked my microscope on the rolltop desk in the corner and the hat rack with the black top hat I wore occasionally. So what if I tried to replicate Sherlock Holmes' living room? It worked for me.

Jan's concern was that there wasn't much money searching for lost pets and my time would be better spent at a 'Real Job' like being a mailman or working for a big box store, two occupations I'd tried but found deeply unsatisfying. Nowadays my part-time gig as a voice actor in commercials helped cover expenses if work in the pet rescue world was slow. Producers loved my English accent. I was considered the go-to guy for Mrs. Compton's Magnificent Marmalade.

I sat back and glanced at the report Jan had left. I'd tracked down a poodle named Lulu who'd taken up with a bloodhound named Rex in southwest Minneapolis and all was well. I was contemplating what the resulting puppies would look like when Jan stepped into my office.

'Phone call,' she said, pointing to the light blinking on my desk phone. We still had a landline. 'A Mrs. Jorgenson. Something about a missing dog.' She raised her eyebrows and mouthed, *Again*. But she smiled as she went back to her desk. I did too. Arguing with her made me realize how much I liked my job. And Jan. Not everyone was so fortunate.

I picked up the receiver. 'Simon Hope here,' I said. 'How can I help?'

I listened, interjecting occasionally, taking notes all the while. When she was done speaking, I summarized our conversation: 'So, your Pomeranian doggy Snuffy ran off last night and you're worried. You live west of Minneapolis near Lake Minnetonka. Is that correct?'

'Yes. I'm incredibly concerned. Coyotes have been sighted in our area.'

I said, soothingly, 'Please don't worry, Mrs.

Jorgenson. I'll be out there within the hour and start the search. I'm sure I can find Snuffy.'

'Oh, thank you!'

I stepped to my coat rack, put on my tweet jacket and my Sherlock Holmes deerstalker cap. I was all set. I headed out the door. The game was afoot. Snuffy was loose and needed to be found before something horrible happened to her. I was just the man for it.

I adjusted my cap and waved to Jan as I walked out the door. If she rolled her eyes, I didn't notice. I was already on the hunt.

# Saturday Sample: And I Said, Connie

**Linda Morse**

*a nice cup of tea*

**Nursing Home. Connie, a very elderly lady, sits in bed. She can neither communicate nor move. The monologue is taking place in her head.**

*(Connie sits up normally and speaks initially as if to a Care Assistant.)*

Go away. Not today. Fly, fly, bye-bye. Buy time, my time, time place. My space.

See the floor grow into the walls. Crawl up the walls. Bright, sight, sun light through coloured glass. Turquoise, kingfisher blue. Fine shine, taffeta silk sheen on the walls. Gleam on the walls.

They don't know there's a mouse. Comes to chat, look at that no cat, when it's quiet… Someone drops crumbs on my bed. House mouse knows. Whiskers them away. Nibbles. Nibbles.

Pretty pink hands.

*(Mimics Care Assistant)* 'Here we are, Connie. Nice cup of tea.'

It's not a cup, give up, upper cup, upper cut. It's a beaker leaker. Thing you give to babies. Don't think I'll drink. Not going to sink to that.

*(Mimics Care Assistant)* 'Here we are.'

Clear, we are here. Too near. I wish you weren't. Interrupts my flow. Go. No, the silly woman comes in with her 'Here we are's' and 'Nice cups of tea'. Can't she see, I'm busy… organising my party.

*(Mimics Care Assistant)* 'See you later.'

You might. You might not. I might go out. Go out like a light. Give you a fright…

That'll thwart you, caught you, taught you, teach you teacher, preacher and your beaker leaker.

SILENCE

Don't like this blanket. Smells of mould and cold. I'm old. They told me, I'm old. Held a 'do'. How d'you do? Hullabaloo. My space was full of bodies. No idea who they were. Who's there? Don't care. Want some peace. 'This is your niece' Bluebell, Tinkerbell, Mirabelle, Daisybelle, or some dingling, dangling, jingling, jangle-spangled old person come on the day, all the way from New Zealand… or Wales.

A hundred. Telegram and foolish man… kept repeating, 'Century not out', 'Century not out'. Something about… football anyway. Any way at all.

He wasn't tall.

*(She hears the Care Assistant enter.)*

Door creak, smell leak, piss reek. Why do you enter my place in the world of my own making a noise?

*(Mimics Care Assistant)* 'Time to take your tablets, Connie.'

No.

Didn't take 'em yesterday, pesterday or the day before the war. Don't pretend anymore. Won't wait anymore to spit 'em out till after she's gone.

There. Learn who's who. What will you do? Who's boss? She's cross and I don't care a toss of the head of the bed.

*(The Care Assistant forces a tablet into her mouth.)*

*(Mimics Care Assistant)* 'Come on Con, don't be difficult.'

Mmmm *(appears to swallow the tablet)*

She's gone.

*(She spits.)*

Don't call me Con.

SILENCE

Face in the rug, smug rug – beady, black eyes and a long nose. Mother called it 'aquiline'. Very fine. She tried to better herself.

Here come my guests, not pest guests. Interesting people. Come by invitation, conversation, witty, pretty, ditty people. No tablets and beaker leakers. Respect me, directly address me correctly as Constance or Mrs. Brown.

*(Connie gets up to welcome her guests.)*

Hello. Welcome.

*(She fusses with her skirt, as if having received a compliment.)*

Thank you. I bought it last week. New. Turquoise, kingfisher blue. Fine shine, taffeta silk sheen. Be seen. Be Queen of the night. Bright in the light, glittering sight, sweet delight.

Frank. So glad you could come. The party wouldn't be the same.

*(She becomes coquettish.)* The dancing will start soon and swoon and over the moon.

Let's stand a moment together forever watching the rest in the glow and the flow and the show.

*(She giggles as she talks to Frank and points out other guests.)*

Look at his whiskers. He has such beady eyes, aquiline nose, smart clothes and his spouse mouse has pretty pink hands?

Help yourself to crumbs. Nibbles. Nibbles.

PAUSE

MUSIC (*Cheek to Cheek* Fred Astaire)

Ah, the music's playing, swaying. First dance, first glance, last chance.

My oldest friend… in our timeless place. Handsome face. Grace and lace.

Last dance, last glance, last chance.

*(She dances, as if with a partner. When the music finishes, she is breathless.)*

MUSIC FADES.

You've worn me out… but you haven't lost your touch. Such touch, so much touching, moving… moving away.

*(She greets another guest.)*

Ruby, I'm so glad you came. Yes, it's sad. Nothing lasts forever and a day.

Be nice to stay, but we're leaving as soon as the party's over. To live in clover… nearly over…

*(Connie returns to bed.)*

Must you all go so soon… we've just begun… in the sun. It's set and there's hardly a moon… so soon… over so soon…

*(Connie stops breathing.)*

# Saturday Sample, Ways of Seeing

## Rick Vick

### *old wine*

He watches her, at first vaguely – an old woman paddling. So he sees her through his seven year old eyes – although she is no more than forty, a few years older than his mother. She is standing in the tattered lace of the wave's furthest reach up the beach. She is alone. Not just by herself, he thinks, having some notion of what alone means, being an only child. Something about her stillness keeps his eyes fixed on her. She is not like the mothers and a few fathers further up the beach, beyond the breakwater, ankle deep in the cold North sea, keeping eyes on their children, further out, splashing and screaming with abandon.

As he watches he senses a tremor in her body as she lifts her head and stares out to sea. He follows her gaze to the distant smudge of the horizon. There is not much to see; no boats just the undulations of the waves. She is wearing a dark red dress which, unlike the other women in the shallows, she has not gathered in her hand to lift.

She steps forward and keeps on moving, slowly, into the incoming waves. He glances towards his mother, who is unpacking triangles of sandwiches and three bananas from two plastic boxes, laying them on a small square of white cloth. He is about to call her attention to the woman but seeing the tight line of her mouth decides against disturbing her. His father had said he would not come on the picnic outing as he had a fiver on the 4.15 at Doncaster. She had not been pleased.

She is up to her thighs when he looks back. Something in him knows what she is doing but he has not the language to put his intuition into words. Deeper and deeper she goes, the sea up almost to her waist. The dress has risen up around her. Like a dingy come to rescue her, he thinks.

She lifts her hand to her head and frees a clasp or pin that holds the long dark hair that falls to her shoulders.

On and on she pushes. He feels her effort. She stops. The ocean heaves all around her body up to her chest. He looks up the beach. No one has seen her. He wants to shout out, to point but does not.

Quite suddenly she raises her arms, fingers outstretched, and dips under the water and is gone. Just like that. He hugs his knees hard in his arms, staring. Staring so hard – willing her to reappear. She does not.

No one else has noticed. He looks around. All is just as it was the last time he had looked and he wonders if he had seen, truly seen, what he had seen.

# AUGUST

# The Void

## Mia McNamara

***hot tea of any kind***

No more fog and no chill breeze that coaxed her tanned skin. No more colour; no more air.

She feared for her life.

No longer did she have a feeling of security; no longer did she wish she ventured into the forest alone. The air was hot, it charred her lungs – it was even thicker than before, suffocating the young woman every time she tried to catch her breath.

Screams could be heard in the distance, but no matter where she looked, the source of the screams could not be found. Everything was black; smoky. The only thing she could see was the occasional flicker of small, bright red orbs illuminating the darkness. Two orbs would appear, then two orbs would disappear; four orbs would appear, then four orbs would disappear; eight orbs would appear – more would appear, then disappear. Twenty, forty, one hundred – the young woman lost count. They were appearing faster than she could count. Wherever she turned, the orbs were there, flashing in the dark.

The second the young woman blinked, a yelp of pain escaped her lips. Something from behind – something lurking in the dark – had reached out and clawed her. At that moment, she knew; she knew that those red orbs were not orbs, but something more sinister. There were thousands of eyes staring into her soul, watching her, observing her. They were stalking her like prey.

The young woman's knees collapsed as another attack came from her right. She was in a nightmare. The eyes were blinking faster than before, and a deep, scratchy laugh came from the distance.

'I know you can hear me, Irene,' someone said. The moment the voice appeared, the laughter ceased. The young woman rose to her feet and looked around, but the darkness proved to be too thick. 'Looking for this?' the voice asked. What emerged from the shadows was a sight that made the woman's eyes grow wide; horrified. Not too far in front of her was a figure. She couldn't tell what it was. The only visible physiques she could see were large, branch-like structures sticking out at the top of the figure. Everything about the figure was clouded; almost like there was black smoke radiating from it. The young woman backed away in fear, unaware of how the figure managed to steal her dagger. She tried to back away as far as she could, but an abrupt force made her freeze in place.

The figure, on the other hand, moved closer, revealing a leg-shaped shadow with each movement. Legs, arms, and then a head emerged from the cluttered, smoky abyss while maintaining its shadowed presence.

'Don't you dare,' Irene said. She tried to sound threatening, but her shaky voice only received a laugh from the figure. The young woman's body felt paralyzed; she was afraid, and the figure knew that. Irene tried to move, but no matter how hard she tried, not an inch was able to break free. The only thing that was moving was her heart, beating one million times a second.

'Do not be alarmed,' the figure said. 'My Imps had the intention to harm you and take your life; however, I have no intent to harm you – that is, as long as you comply.' The young woman didn't know what to say – not that she could say anything. The voice was coming from the shadowed figure, but she could not tell from where. It felt like it was directly in her ear, yet at the same time, just inches from her face. Then, it disappeared.

Life was restored to the young woman's body. She tried to run, but she just fell to the ground. She twisted, searching for the figure that was just in front of her. 'Let me go!' she said.

'I thought we had an agreement, Irene,' the voice said. This time, she could feel its presence behind her, just inches from her neck. The darkness grew warm as the laughter returned. With every passing second, the laughter grew louder, and the presence behind her was gone.

'Wait, I'm sorry!' Irene said. She tried to explain her actions, but the laughter grew louder. It wasn't until the laughter was in her ear when she, just like before, felt something sharp clawing at her legs.

A dark chuckle came from the darkness. 'Imps, take her,' the voice said. It was at that moment Irene knew her life would be no more, and that she would be one with the darkness.

# On the Spur

Niall Crowley

### *instant coffee*

Matthew loves trains, the best and only way to travel. The onboard tannoy alerts, engines discharge and the carriage shudders into life. He sits back into the release, massaged by the rhythm, pleased with his decision. Once out of the tunnel, shifting terrain demands his attention, nose pressed to the window. Houses shoulder to shoulder and car cluttered arteries transform into scruffy pasture and tracery of hedgerows. There's company at his table, though that can be a mixed blessing.

It was spur of the moment, not put in the diary as required, and not shared with anyone. He was on one of his wanders, passing by the station. Kate came crashing into his head and his heart scrambled humdrum thoughts into long-erased desires. Memories of picking her up off the train, that must have set him off. Whimsical weekends to be played out just for them. Too long. He needed to see her, be with her. The Free Travel Pass, and the few euro for a cup of coffee and the newspaper, were enough to get him on his way. That was all they left him with these days.

She has the look of his grandmother, the woman across the table. The hair done in bleached curls, the make-up generous in its application, and the disciplined order to her outfit. It's as if it is his granny sat opposite, watching over him again. There's that same distant strained look in her eyes, not quite in tune with an amiable facial expression. As if holding back a store of pain. An inevitable fate, pain, once time has had its say. He knows that now. His granny had gone that way early, forever mourning a soulmate taken too young.

Every summer, as soon as the school gates closed, he'd be packed onto the train. Hair blown wild in the wind as the train rattled gleefully across the country. That's his memory of it. Granny would be waiting, dutifully to attention beside her grey Morris Minor, those sad eyes set behind the smile that drew him to her. Always in the same place, just by the station door, a woman of stoic and insistent habit. Not one for hugs, she would usher him straight into the back seat without ceremony.

He'd be swept out of the city to that special place where the sun was ever high in the bluest of skies. Beaches of warm sand spread below her house, where foaming waves would flush up and around to tickle his toes. Car locked safely in the garage, bag deposited in his bedroom, they'd head straight to Mrs Forde's sweet shop. Purposeful and without need for discussion, holiday money to hand. That first sherbet lolly of the summer was always the best. His granny would have one too. For the occasion she'd say. There wasn't a summer would pass before a formal letter would be issued to his mother, seeking further funds to maintain the supply of sherbet lollies.

He realises he's staring at the woman now, bent forward staring, which is embarrassing. It's an unpleasant habit, though not meant to be rude or intrusive. The eyes lock onto the subject, then the head wanders off to explore whatever has been sparked, forgetful of the eyes left fixed and that they might discomfit. She tilts her head and frowns a smile of inquiry at him. He straightens up and coughs in awkwardness. He can't help himself then, just blurts it out.

'You know, you're the spit of my granny. It's bringing me back.'

She barks out a choking laugh, startling him. 'Well aren't you the right playboy. All the best chat up lines.' She chortles more gently, shaking her head. 'That's a winner for sure.'

He's confused, not sure what to make of her. 'No, no. My apologies. I don't mean to be forward. On the contrary, I'm married. I'm actually off up to see my Kate.'

A shout of laughter physically pushes him back in his seat. 'Well, that's nice for you. You'll have a lovely time there for sure.'

He reaches for his newspaper, discomfited, as if patted on the head like the good little boy. The Irish Examiner, that's what they call it these days, but it would ever be the Cork Examiner. His granny had initiated him into its allure. They would take turns of an evening, to read the latest news to each other. A chance to explore the world around and broaden that vocabulary of yours, she used to say. The spread of the broadsheet allows a retreat now, from the intricacies of interpersonal encounter. He stares listlessly, though, at the print in front of him. There's little of interest in it these days. Still, he could never free himself of that daily purchase.

Flowers, he should have got flowers. Kate loves flowers. There had been beds of them she proudly tended around the house. She would roam the fields nearby gathering her pick, taking cuttings for the garden. He had always brought flowers, back when they were courting, just to provoke that slow gentle smile of hers. Not the manicured bouquets on offer from the shop, but wild and messy arrangements, carefully composed from the finest those fields had to offer. That suited her style, captured her spontaneity, mirrored her untamed charm. He can feel his face beaming, gone foolish with the memory. The past is generous sometimes. He knows he'll get an earful for arriving empty handed, though. She's never one to hold back her disapproval, nor, in fairness, her approval on those rare occasions he had got things right enough to earn it.

A young one sits in beside him. She flashes out her phone and is immediately lost to the world around, rapt in her attention to its imperatives. Two thumbs flicker deftly across the screen. Hard to tell if she's composing messages for transmission or interacting with distractions offered by the machine itself. He used to have a phone. He's no technophobe, but they determined it put him at risk of fraud. What there was to defraud him of, he could not tell. He peers over her shoulder to see what has her so absorbed He had never managed such furious dexterity with his phone, nor succumbed to its attractions beyond the purely functional. Feeling that stare clicking in, he pulls himself back in behind the folds of his newspaper.

Kate and himself had to make do with the landline. Cables hoisted on poles stretching across the land to truck words of wistful passion from one side of the country to the other. An amount spent on their transport too. They had met one summer outside Mrs Forde's. Of an age then to have inherited his granny's house, he had still not lost his fondness for the sherbet lollies and the memories they tugged at. She was down visiting friends and out for an explore. Choc-ices were her little addiction, she had confessed. Backs to the warmth of the shop wall, watching over a twinkling bay, they chatted with, for him, unaccustomed ease. Urgent affinity had flourished in their frivolous banter.

On the spur he had asked for her number as she roused herself to leave. Unaccountable temerity had him all of a stutter. She had gently teased as to why he might be needing her number. In the absence of any coherent answer, she had thrown it out over her shoulder as she marched off on her explore. No pencil to hand, he had to recite that number, over and over and over, as he hurried back up the hill to his granny's house. His house then, of course, that had taken some getting used to. A relationship, hanging perilously on the thread of an ever-faulty memory, had survived.

When he wakes, it is with a jolt. He sees they are four around the table now. The three of them are watching him, seems like sternly. Even the young one has deserted her phone to glare alarm in his direction. He stares back, going for dignified denial, though he knows he must have been snoring. They have him on some sort of oxygen tank by night, impossible to sleep with a mask strapped to your face. Sleep apnoea, they pronounce with gravity, puts him at risk, so precautions are to be taken, like it or not. The newcomer hooks his attention, a city slicker with suit and tie, and one of those flashy computers set up in front of him. It triggers his own man of the land temper, a disposition held fiercely to counter those expectations he had failed to meet as a young man. Even as his parents had despaired, so his granny had surely rejoiced from up above.

'You had us worried there, man, you weren't breathing' the newcomer said.

'Are you alright? You've gone all pale on us,' his granny interjected.

The young one was back on her phone, more urgent tasks to hand.

Disconcerted at the interrogation, despite patent sympathy. Aggravated by the dapper moniker of 'man'. He raises his arms. 'I'm grand.' Lowers them to insist. 'Not a bother.' Palms spread for added effect. 'Just dropped off.' He roots around his seat for the newspaper, in search of some dignity. How long had he slept? It can't be far now to the station. She would be there waiting, for sure. She always was, ever would be. The best moment of any journey, arriving into that embrace. He settles in behind the paper, restored by the prospect.

The station is a confusing clatter. Shrill shouts and rasping machinery. People crowd the platform, pushing their way through and out towards the barrier. He has to hold still, tight up against a steel column, just to get his breath and gather his wits. She would be up there by the barrier. There's an expectant crowd milling around it. Watching out for loved ones and waving noisy greetings their direction. He sees her. She's there. He caught a flash of that bobbed black hair of hers. He's ready, all good now.

The barrier negotiated, the crowd parts before him and he strides over to where he saw her. Not a sign of her. Puzzled, he stands alert, peering intently from side to side. The crowd swirls around him. What's she up to? It's not a good time for games and tricks. Maybe she spotted him empty handed. He catches sight of her red coat over by the coffee stall. Relief assails and he heads over with conviction. The woman in the red coat is not Kate, though, doesn't even have her black hair. He's losing it. Ah, there she is, waving frantically at him from the ticket machine. He stumbles over towards her, excitement at bay, anxiety heavy across his shoulders. Closer inspection kills hope, it's another stranger.

He finds an empty seat, sweating with the nerves. He has to sit down. She would come. She always meets him at the station. He should ring her. He can remember her number, rare for him, but the days of the landline are gone. What to do? He's trembling now, bent over to hold his head in his hands for calm. There's still the Free Travel Pass and the train back south, even without the few Euro for a cup of coffee. But that way lies recapture by care, and even punishment for reckless flight. Where is Kate? He needs her, has to be with her.

'You're looking a bit shook up there. Has something happened? Can I help?'

His granny is standing over him, lips pursed, frowning concern through those overburdened eyes. He needs a moment to decipher the question posed.

'I'm waiting. I'm waiting for Kate. She's my wife, I told you. Always meets me at the station. It's fine, it'll be fine.'

'Hmmph. Is there a number you could ring?'

He looks in puzzlement at her. She doesn't get it, times have changed. The landline doesn't work anymore. She looks exasperated back at him. He shrinks at patent disapproval. Moments of distress have a nasty habit of conjuring up memories he has carefully packed away to avoid scrutiny. The past can be cruel betimes. He can almost hear the scream, see the lights of the onrushing truck, feel his paralysis and inability to react.

'It was on the spur of the moment. Our anniversary, a fancy meal and all the trappings. We were headed over to that forest above the village for the romance of a full-moon. I shouldn't have been driving.' Head bowed again, he peers up at his granny, pleading for absolution.

# Just Two Days

Gill James

***vintage champagne***

'I'll be blunt. You have just two days' worth of oxygen left. We're truly sorry.' The commander's face was grey and he was frowning slightly.

'Thanks for letting me know.' This sort of end had always been on the cards. They were prepared. That was why his salary was so high and his pension would carry on at exactly the same rate. At least Susie and the kids would be fine.

'Make yourself really comfortable. Shall we keep in touch?'

Brad shook his head. 'No, it would just be a reminder.'

'Al right. Call us up if you need anything. And we suggest instigating protocol 500 in thirty-six hours.'

'Will do.'

The vintage champagne had been supplied for when the centre was fully open. Well, that wasn't going to happen now. After three quarters of the bottle he began to feel a little light-headed. Best get something to eat.

The smoked salmon and caviar were just right.

He watched his favourite old films noir: *The Wolf Man, Le Corbeau* and *Arsenic and Old Lace.*

He wrote a long letter to Susie and slightly shorter ones to Beth and Sam.

Thirty-three hours passed really quickly. He looked at the instructions for protocol 500. He would just have to attach the tube to the permacanula. They suggested then lying down and listening to music of his choice. Simple enough really. He had a play list of soothing classics. That would do nicely.

He broke open the sterile packaging and was just about to insert the tube when the communicator buzzed. The commander again.

'Hold fire, Jackson. We've rectified the fault and your oxygen supply will be back to normal in two hours.'

# SEPTEMBER

# Queen of the Lazy Leopard

**Frank Zahn**

***a glass of white wine***

Middle-aged single people in Omaha came to the Lazy Leopard every Friday and Saturday night in an attempt to ease their loneliness. It was a dimly lit cocktail lounge with backlit photos of leopards in repose on the walls, an L-shaped bar, round tables with comfy chairs, and a dance floor with overhead star lights. A combo and a singer with quivering cleavage provided forties and fifties music for slow dance and swing.

The woman who everyone called The Queen out of earshot sat at the same table each night. She always dressed impeccably in red, purple, or black silk or chiffon with pearls and sling heels. Although born and brought up in Omaha's seedy and notorious southside, her fine features, porcelain skin, pampered raven hair, and composure gave her the look of an aristocrat – a queen. And that's why the moniker, The Queen.

Her most captivating feature was her Mona Lisa smile and glow, which beguiled and drove men to ask for a dance, and while dancing, invariably ask if she would have coffee or maybe breakfast with them later when the music stopped and the bartenders sounded last-call.

The Queen loved to dance, but when a man held

her too close on the dance floor or let his hand slip below her waist, she was quick to react. She grimaced and pushed him away with a few caustic words. Then she retreated to the ladies' room to refresh herself and regain her composure.

Her trips to the ladies' room for whatever reason were always a treat for the men who sat along the long end of the bar. As she passed by, they turned their heads and ogled the sensual movement of her body inside her silk or chiffon attire until she disappeared from view.

Invariably, one of the men would say something like, 'Now that's my kind of woman,' or, 'I'd give my right arm for one night in the sack with that piece of cake,' or, 'I'd sure like to be The Queen's king for a couple of nights.'

Ruthie, who was several of the men's last resort, Martha, a recent divorcee with attitude and Laverne, an art teacher with beady eyes and loose skin were among the women who came to The Queen's table to say hello, gossip, and make sarcastic remarks about others in the place, especially the men.

All three of them dressed to impress not only each other but also the short supply of men, especially those who had jobs, didn't have body odour or dirty fingernails, and acted as if they could be controlled with a home-cooked dinner and a roll in the hay every now and then.

Sometimes, Laverne lingered at The Queen's table

and waited for a man to ask her for a dance other than Tony, a runt of a man from South Omaha with mafia pretensions. When that didn't happen, she gave Tony the nod to meet her on the dance floor.

The Queen showed no romantic interest in any of the men, except for Michael Rosellini, a tall and broad-shouldered man who always sported a dark suit with a white shirt and a yellow or red power tie. Although he didn't show up every Friday or Saturday night, she came alive when he did, quickly losing herself in his masterful charm and good-humour. And he was the only man she would leave with after the bartenders sounded last call.

On the Friday night before the Lazy Leopard closed for good and a crew of men brought in a wrecking ball, a man came to The Queen's table and asked her to dance. She had never seen him before, but he was handsome, trim, and well dressed. So, she obliged.

On the dance floor, the man immediately pulled her close to him and held her tight. She struggled to free herself, but the man would not let go.

Michael, who had arrived and stood at the bar watching her and the man on the dance floor, rushed to her aid. He grabbed the man's shoulder and said, 'Let her go.'

'Get lost,' the man said, dancing away from Michael with The Queen still in his grasp.

Michael followed. He grabbed the man's shoulder again. 'I said, let her go!'

The man released his grasp on The Queen. Then he turned, raised his fist, and took a swing at Michael. Michael dodged the swing and punched the man squarely on the jaw. The man stumbled backward but regained his footing.

The music stopped. The Queen and the other couples on the dance floor backed away from the man and Michael. They looked on in dismay.

Michael lunged at the man, his fists raised and ready to throw a second punch.

Rage filled the man's eyes. He pulled a revolver from a holster inside his suit jacket, aimed it at Michael, and fired two shots.

Michael grabbed the left side of his chest. He fell backward and collapsed onto the dance floor. Blood oozed through his fingers and quickly soaked his clothing.

The man turned and ran in panic toward the exit, motioning with the revolver for people to get out of his way.

'Call the police!' someone shouted.

'And call an ambulance!' someone else added.

As people gathered around Michael, The Queen dropped to her knees beside him. She cradled his head in her lap.

'I love you, Michael,' she said with tears in her eyes. 'I love you so much.'

Michael tried to speak but managed only to whisper her name before closing his eyes and taking a final breath.

The police arrived and questioned The Queen and others. An ambulance arrived as well and removed Michael's body after an okay from the police officer in charge.

Several days later, The Queen attended the memorial service for Michael along with only a few of the people who frequented the Lazy Leopard on Friday and Saturday nights. A couple of days after that, the wrecking ball did its job, and huge trucks hauled away the debris. The Lazy Leopard was no more, and the people who frequented it on Friday and Saturday nights scattered and became part of a dozen other nightspots that catered to middle-aged singles.

The man who shot and killed Michael Rosellini was never found.

And no one saw or heard from The Queen again. She locked herself away in her Old Market condominium and consoled herself with memories of Michael and her Friday and Saturday nights in the Lazy Leopard. She had groceries and the other things she needed delivered and left at her door.

Memories of her faded along with the night the man shot and killed Michael Rosellini. Memories of relationships, places, and events invariably fade into the past. And when the relationships are superficial, as they often are in a cocktail lounge, memories of them fade more quickly.

# Autonomic, Again

## Steve Gerson

### *Bloody Mary*

'I'm sorry, Jennie,' he said, again, for the twentieth time that week, maybe for the twentieth time that hour. He'd lost track.

She shook her head, saying, 'Your sorries don't work anymore, Jack. They're like the loose change I find under the couch cushions, next to lint and dead skin. You say it so often that it's like your breaths taken, your heartbeats, without thought, without feeling. It's autonomic, Jack.'

'I'm sor…' he almost said, his autonomic reflexes sparking in spasms. He had become a jangle of ganglia, more random nerve cells than sentient being. 'Jennie, I mean it. No more. It'll never happen again. Honest.'

'Autonomic,' she said. 'Do you even know what you're sorry for this time?'

He paused, as if stuck at a crossroad with oncoming traffic, all targeted toward colliding with him. As if he were an addled air traffic controller at Heathrow with 50 planes stacking up to land in heavy fog. 'Uh.' He paused again, running through possibilities, then mentally ticking off items like a cashier at a checkout lane. Maybe this sorry was because he kept talking at the movie yesterday, peeving those around him. Maybe because he left the kitchen light on all night, again. Maybe because he kept her awake with his snoring, but how would he know? He was asleep, damn it. How was he supposed to control himself during REM moments? Maybe because he lost $100 at poker last Tuesday with his buddies (really it was $250, a tiny lie, he thought). Maybe because he had covertly ogled the cute waitress at Sunday brunch when she delivered his third Bloody Mary with an extra shot of vodka and two strips of bacon. Maybe because he forgot Jennie's birthday, again, but she always said she hated getting older. He just didn't want to remind her. 'I was being thoughtful,' he said out loud, autonomically, more like an involuntary hiccup than a reasoned thought.

'What?' Jennie asked. 'Thoughtful? Wishful thinking Jack. That's the problem. Thoughtlessness is more your speed. In fact, that's all I'm asking for, thoughtfulness. Think of me, Jack, not just yourself.'

'I'm sorry, Jennie,' he said, again, for the twentieth time that week, maybe for the twentieth time that hour.

# When We Watch The Lord of the Rings Movies Back to Back (Extended Edition)

**Hannah Retallick**

***old-fashioned with popcorn syrup***

We watched Frodo trudge to Mordor on one of the rare days he was with me instead of her. A bowl rested between us, crammed with popcorn, sweet and salty because he can never commit. Frodo leant on his faithful companion. I sucked my fingers clean, waved them towards the screen.

True love right there, I said.

He didn't show he'd heard. Maybe he hadn't. Still, we kept watching, silently, eleven hours straight, stopping only three times to refresh ourselves and shake our bodies awake.

My crossed leg switched sides every few minutes, proving it didn't care either way. When it was towards him, I slipped into his sofa rut. The empty popcorn bowl was the only thing separating my hand from his burning arm. Summer or winter, his sun-speckled skin runs as hot as Mount Doom. I feel it, she feels it, we all feel it, drawn together in voiceless fellowship; a fellowship we pretend doesn't exist, because we're 'not like other girls'.

He was yawning by the time the credits rolled. He checked his phone, perhaps looking for a message from one of the others, but who knows? He had made it none of my business.

I longed to watch the extra features, make a weekend of it, but I didn't ask. I couldn't. It would have thrown us straight into the lava, hurried our inevitable end. At least for now, he was here, and we were safe.

# The Consequences of Ambition

## Maria Kinnersley

***an americano, fairly strong***

No one could have foreseen the consequences of the well-intentioned but misguided actions of a science student, leading to one act which had the potential to change the world forever.

Sally was relieved to obtain temporary work during the summer break. She needed the money. Student loans didn't cover all her needs. Some extra cash would be welcome. After three terms of studying biological science and biochemistry at a college near to her home in Liverscombe, she looked forward to putting her knowledge into practice.

*Of course,* she thought, *I'm not naive enough to think I've got all the answers, but working in this biochemical research facility is going to give me Brownie points and experience. And who knows? I may be around when there is an exciting discovery. I might even find it myself.*

The job she managed to obtain involved her working in a small laboratory researching methods of recycling plastics using bacteria.

'These investigations have been going on for many years,' said Professor Andrews to the starry-eyed girl, as he showed her around on her first day. 'It's just not commercially viable at present.'

'Why is that?' she asked.

'The concentration of bacteria needs to be stronger,' he answered. 'On a small scale it works. We need to look to larger scale methods using more powerful organisms. And…'

'Yes,' she responded breathlessly.

'Nothing you need to know at present. Your job won't involve that kind of work. You'd need to be vetted and have had previous experience.'

She looked down to hide the disappointment, but he noted her action and smiled benignly.

'All I was going to say was that we haven't yet been successful in producing strains of organisms that are specific to types of plastic… the types we want to get rid of. Imagine what would happen if it weren't.'

'Oh,' was all she could think of to say.

Every morning she was up early, bursting with energy and ready to get to work. At night, she would pour over research papers and take notes. If only, she thought, I could discover the right organism. They may take me on when I've done my time in college.

In truth, the job that she was doing there was menial. Others were conducting the trials. Her work involved preparing the chemicals and substrates for the different micro-organisms they were evaluating, all of which took place in a protected environment. Then when the results came through, she inputted the information on a computer database.

She tried to persuade herself that the work she was doing was valuable. In chats to her friends from college on WhatsApp, she boasted about the laboratory, making it sound as though she was heavily involved in the experimentation process. In truth, she found what she was doing boring and repetitive. One of the lab workers smiled when she expressed her frustrations.

'We've all been there, Sally,' he said. 'It's a necessary part of your learning process. Most science can be boring, but that's how we get to know what works and what doesn't.'

Her confidence was knocked but she hoped that one day her skills would be put to use in this work, resulting in good news for the world. The elimination of waste plastic.

'And kudos for me,' she whispered as she dozed in bed at the end of another mundane day.

Not long after, there came a day of great excitement. One of the professor's assistants, an earnest looking lanky individual called Harold came running into the computer room where a moody Sally was slowly typing in data.

'He's done it,' he yelled.

'Done what?' she asked.

Harold swallowed and looked at her. Then he spoke slowly as if explaining to a child.

'The prof has sorted another piece of the puzzle,' he explained. 'We're getting very close to finding out the answers.'

'Does that mean you'll be carrying out field studies soon?'

He smiled condescendingly. 'I think we're a little way off that. But…' He tapped his nose. 'I'll let you know when we do.'

*I think I'm going to be friends with him,* Sally thought. *He could help me.*

The summer came and went. Sally went back to college, but not before receiving a request from Professor Andrews to come back and help during her holidays.

'We're very pleased with your work,' he said. 'We can always find room for conscientious workers like you.' Sally glowed with happiness.

When she returned to the laboratory, Harold was still working there, with his freckles and copper wavy hair. She cultivated their relationship. They regularly met for coffee and lunches at the canteen, where she ensured the conversation always veered round to the progress of the testing of the plastic eating bacteria.

Midway through her second summer, and after much badgering, Harold took her one lunchtime to the laboratory where the different strains of bacteria were stored. She stood at one of the tables, enthralled at the sight of banks of small labelled vials as the young technician kept watch for other staff coming in.

'This is a secret between you and me,' he said. 'You mustn't tell anyone else. I could get into a lot of trouble.'

'What are these?' she asked pointing at the vials.

'They're the strains of bacteria we're assessing now. Don't touch,' he whispered urgently as she reached forward. 'You could contaminate them.'

Sally allowed herself to be ushered out of the room, but not before she had taken note of the size and shape of the vials.

A couple of weeks later, she persuaded Harold to let her visit again.

'Promise me you won't touch anything,' he said.

With her fingers crossed behind her back, she nodded solemnly.

As she stood in the laboratory once more, thrilling to the scale of works taking place, Harold's mobile rang. With a warning glance at her, he turned his back and took the call. Moments later, he turned back and looked suspiciously at her.

'That was a strange call,' he said. 'The caller hung up when I answered.'

She returned his gaze with an innocent expression. Inside she was elated that her ruse had worked out. She was able to exchange the vial with one similar she had brought with her. Now she could conduct scientific work of her own.

That night, she waited until she got home before she removed the vial from her coat pocket. Bringing it to eye level, she examined the contents. It appeared innocuous. Well maybe it is, she thought. It might just be the preparation before the bacteria was impregnated.

‘Well, there’s only one way to find out,’ she muttered.

Reaching under her bed, she brought out a metal container with cut up plastic bottles. Carefully she removed the vial cover and shook out the contents over the material.

With a notebook beside her she took note of the time, then closed the tin, and replaced it.

‘I’ll check again in twenty-four hours,’ she murmured.

The following day, she could not stay still. She completed all her jobs in record time and was helping others, an act unheard of by the others working with her.

Harold popped in at lunch time.

‘Come for a bite to eat?’

Sally shook her head.

‘Not today. I’m not hungry.’

She studied the screen in front of her and did not see his disappointed expression.

Finally, she was able to go home. She ate her dinner with her parents, then quickly went to her room.

Cautiously she opened the container to find it empty.

‘Oh,’ she said, her tone neutral.

She shook the tin. There were no remnants of plastic visible at all and she sat on her bed deep in thought.

‘Well, it works,’ she muttered. ‘I thought there would be something left. Oh well.’

Sally upended the tin and gave it a tap. Unknown to her, in the slight breeze, microscopic bacterial spores drifted out of the open window.

# OCTOBER

# Between the Notes

**Justin Aylward**

***a warmed over americano, for that bitter aftertaste, ideal for this story***

Caitlin stood at the bus stop holding the large cello case, wondering if her boyfriend understood anything she had just said.

It was a Friday in March, and classes were finishing up for the weekend. The other students hurried through the halls as though summer had already arrived.

Kaitlin didn't want to be late for her arrangement, so avoided her friends after the last lecture of the day. She gripped the cello case as the wind tousled her red hair. The bus turned onto the narrow campus road and stopped. It was on time, which was rare, and free of passengers, which was rarer.

Kaitlin lugged the cello case down the passageway as the bus took off. She sat at the back and let the case rest between her knees. She looked out the window across the barren industrial estate to see numerous cement boulders and neglected bags of sand piled up high. These were supposed to be people's homes, but you couldn't even make a shelter out of the material in the state they were in.

Kaitlin turned away, unbuttoned her red woollen coat, and resisted the urge to check her phone.

It was her fifth session at the house, but she

preferred to see them as mini concerts. They were the ideal form of practice, with a quiet audience and a generous fee. If anyone asked she said she was giving lessons, but when she mentioned it to Connor he had a different reaction. It was as though she spoke in a foreign language. He tried to humour her but couldn't dispel the look of embarrassment in his eyes. She knew the more she said, the more awkward it would be.

'I know it sounds odd, but it's not what you think.' She said.

Connor, with shaggy brown hair and a sleepy face, held Kaitlin close, but he couldn't look at her. He wanted to say it was strange and that she probably shouldn't do it, but in the least confrontational manner.

'Is there anyone else there when you're playing?' he asked.

Kaitlin looked up and with a cheeky smile tried to reassure him, but she knew he already had the wrong idea.

'Yes,' she said, 'there's a maid, and his daughter is there too.'

'A maid?' he repeated. 'What is it, Downton Abbey?'

Kaitlin laughed, but the joking only emphasized the awkwardness that would accentuate her departure, and make it seem more like a betrayal than a temporary goodbye.

Connor pulled away as Kaitlin leaned in to kiss

him. The wind blew her hair across his stubbly chin and tickled his mouth. He smiled but couldn't bring himself to look at her directly.

Kaitlin knew that no amount of embellishment could mitigate the feeling of intimacy implicit in a one-to-one performance. What she thought of as a kind gesture, Connor imagined was a sexually charged engagement that reeked of perversity. If he had shown an interest in her music, she might have told him sooner, or it may not have come to this at all. The question had been on her mind since the first session weeks earlier. Before she knew how, she was posing it to him.

'If I went away, how long before you'd forget me?' she asked.

Connor tried to look intrigued with a raised eyebrow but it seemed as though every utterance implied the opposite of what the words meant.

'Why, where are you going?' he asked.

'Nowhere,' she said. 'I was just wondering. What do you think when you think of me?'

This was sounding like a breakup.

Connor pulled back, finally separating himself from Kaitlin's embrace. A sigh escaped between his lips that grew more hurried as he sought a quick exit.

'Is there a right answer to this question?' he asked.

'What do you mean?'

'I feel like you're setting a trap.'

They were only nineteen, and too young to be concerned about a distant future – Connor certainly wasn't – but Kaitlin couldn't help feel like there was nothing memorable between them that would solidify their relationship across time.

'It's not like that,' she said. 'I just…'

Connor picked up his bag and gripped her by the arms.

'Listen, it doesn't matter,' he said, 'I'm not angry or anything.'

'I just thought you should know I'm not sneaking around.'

He zipped up his jacket and kissed her cheek before turning away.

'I get it. We'll talk later, I have to run.' He said.

Before Kaitlin could call after him, he was disappearing among the other students exiting the canteen. He would probably spend the night playing XBOX and guzzling energy drinks. If that didn't go too well, he would go out with friends.

It could be another two days before Kaitlin saw him again. Maybe she would be over it by then, she thought, or maybe he would. She looked at her phone. There were no messages or calls.

The bus left the motorway behind and ascended the bushy hills overlooking the bay.

Five minutes later, Kaitlin exited the bus and carried the cello case up the winding driveway, passed the yacht and blue outhouse. She looked up at the large brick façade and Viennese windows. There was something antiquated about the grounds that made her feel older. The house was like a secret buried amid the trees and surrounding verdure. Kaitlin wondered how long you had to work before affording a house like it.

Bree opened the front door and smiled, her short black hair and straight teeth as perfect as Kaitlin remembered. She could take a dozen guesses and still not know how old Bree was. Her flowery blouses and satin pants were equally modish and classical. Kaitlin presumed she was a stage actress before taking time out to nurse her father.

'Come in,' she said. 'Dad's just sitting by the fire.'

Kaitlin removed her coat and carried the case down the hall. The smell of smokeless coal and vegetable soup pervaded the house.

'I'll make some tea,' Bree said.

'Thank you,' Kaitlin said.

She entered the reading room, stepping gently on the thick carpet as the fire crackled under the mantle. He sat facing the window in a furnished brown armchair, his rumpled body nestled in the threadbare fabric. She only saw the left side of his white face where the light shone through the window.

'You're back,' he said.

He didn't speak at the end of the previous session, and Kaitlin assumed he was unimpressed. No sad pieces, was his only request. Kaitlin thought there were no other pieces you could play on the cello, as it produced a uniquely haunted sound. But he never complained. It was easy to appease an audience with Bach if you played properly, and Kaitlin never doubted herself.

'Sorry I'm late,' she said.

The man did not respond, but sat silently facing the window.

Kaitlin lifted the cello from the case and walked to the hardwood chair a few metres behind him. From where she sat the sun appeared to set in front the man's chair. She didn't want to put him asleep but thought he wouldn't need any help.

There was a notebook and pen on the small table beside the window apron, and ornamental picture frames on the bureau drawer. Kaitlin wanted to look more closely at the woman in the black and white photograph, but didn't want to invade his space. Other frames showed pictures of children playing, seaside frolics, a wedding party.

He could have asked Bree to buy a radio or record player, but there must have been something about a live performance that stirred him. Kaitlin didn't know and was afraid to ask. She would probably notice new things even on the one-hundredth session, if she lasted that long.

The man made a ruffling noise and cleared his throat. Kaitlin sat forward and noticed he was folding a piece of paper numerous ways.

She waited a moment before playing a few stray notes and gauging the feel of the bow in her hand. He would settle down once she began. Soon she was in the middle of Mendelssohn's first sonata, eyes closed and the feeling of security spreading through her. Kaitlin thought it was an ambivalent piece, suggesting both joy and sadness. She imagined an aging woman finally reuniting with her lover only to realise the passion they shared has diminished. It wasn't the same without piano accompaniment, and the pace was quicker, but still the man was restful.

A few minutes passed and Kaitlin forgot where she was. It was just her and the music. An hour could have passed, or two, she would not have known. It was only when thoughts crept into her mind that she lost concentration, but there was nothing stopping her now. It had been ten minutes since Bree promised to bring tea, but there was no sign of her.

After Mendelssohn, Kaitlin played Rachmaninoff's sonata in G minor. It was contemplative, suggesting nostalgia and gentleness. She played quickly through the piano solos, and soon felt the music envelop her. She was never more aware of herself than when playing and yet the music allowed her to escape the present uncertainty of her life.

There was a mysterious quality to the cello that always appealed to Kaitlin. The first time she heard it, it was as though another piece of her had been added. Composers didn't put their emotion into the music, she thought, but took emotions from it, and shared it with listeners. Communication seemed easier through the instrument.

Now there was another noise, not sudden, but subtle, rising up like a plume of smoke. It was the man, muttering to himself, testing out the words like soup on a spoon. Kaitlin continued playing, but her concentration was lost. She tried to hear what he was saying, but she didn't want to cease playing and draw his attention.

The sun had now disappeared behind the chair and Kaitlin could only see the shadowy outline against the window. She had reached the section where the piano took over the main melody. There was a moment of silence when she heard the man speak louder.

'That's what happened,' he said, 'I'm sure of it.'

He was somewhere else, or in a different time.

Kaitlin wanted to stop. This was the first time she heard him speak during a session. Maybe he wanted something. It became clear as Kaitlin listened that his mind was elsewhere.

'It was after we got back,' he continued. 'You said you would.'

Kaitlin sat quietly with the bow dangling between her fingers. The music had left her, but the echoes remained. She didn't know what the man was talking about, but the insistence of his words rang true. It must have been his wife. Her photograph was on the bureau next to the chair.

Kaitlin thought about Connor. He was probably sitting in the library scrolling through his phone. She wanted to ask him again what he remembered when he thought about her. It was important that she occupy a piece of his mind before the feeling between them soured. He never listened to her play, and she didn't know what else to do about him.

'How could I forget?' the man said. 'We promised each other.'

In the four previous sessions, Kaitlin didn't know what the man wanted from her playing, but now she had made him feel something vital. She wanted to know precisely what it was, and wondered if she inspired the same feeling in anyone else.

Bree knocked on the door, entering without a response.

'Is everything okay?' she asked.

Kaitlin turned fast, and with tears in her eyes tried to find the right words to explain, but there was nothing she could say. The music spoke for itself, and although it wasn't hers, it gave some consolation.

# Whether the Weather

## Lynn Clement

### *a hot toddy*

*The wind is coming tonight,* the flashwall stated in a flat tone.

Ellery assumed even AI was fed up with the same thing day after day. Last night it had been, *the rain is coming tomorrow.* And of course it came. The weather predictor was always correct. Everything was now always correct. Boredom was a fact of life.

The rain gauge attached to the food-room wall, measured 150ml – probably another 150 to go before the rain stopped.

Ellery hoped that the soak in the community space would drain. They hadn't seen Noakes the drain-clearing droid for a while. They studied the community space monitor on the flashwall.

The little red boat was still in its mooring and its roof was intact.

They nodded at the weather monitor and selected – speed of the wind for tomorrow. *One hundred,* it said.

*Mmm,* thought Ellery, *I'd better check the moorings.*

Ellery hadn't been outside for some time and decided to physically check the boat, rather than use the AI. They knew they wouldn't meet anyone else. Most people stayed in their pods during the rains, operating buttons for their every need.

They stood inside the capsule wardrobe and selected rain. Suitable clothing was put on them. They slid down the outside chute labelled 'boat'.

Ellery hit the dockside with a bump. The floating pontoon was a lot higher than the computer setting realized. They would have to adjust that when back in their pod. The pontoon bobbled about in the already swollen moat. The rain pattered on the metal boards. Ellery slipped and slid towards the edge of the pontoon.

'Hey, what are you doing?' The voice came from the P.A. system built into the wall of the pod.

It was a masculine voice, definitely not AI. Ellery hadn't heard one of them for a while. There weren't many cis men around nowadays.

'You – why are you out of your pod?' the voice questioned in a demanding tone.

Ellery didn't answer; they were too busy clinging on to the boat which they had now slammed up against.

'I'm coming down, stay there,' said the masculine voice.

Ellery thought, *definitely not a robot, they're not stupid enough to say* – 'Stay there!'

A figure clad in yellow rainwear quickly approached them.

*He's staying upright.* They felt their feminine hormones surging.

The man pulled Ellery up by their arms and held them in a bear hug. He walked towards the suckchute and waved his hand. The weather-guard swooshed open. Still holding Ellery tightly, he stood inside the chute.

'New sucker-boots,' he said to Ellery, as they looked at his feet. 'Maybe you need to get some.'

'Do they do them in pink?' Ellery asked looking for the man's eyes.

'A question you'll have to ask your dresser,' he said. Putting Ellery down, he held out his gloved hand.

'Gormond,' he said.

'How delightfully old-fashioned of you,' said Ellery taking his hand.

The chute sucked and threw Ellery forward towards the man's chest. He smelled good. Musk and lavender mix. Their favourite.

'Ellery,' they said. 'We're pleased to meet you.'

'I'm the new pod-keeper,' announced the man, removing his visored helmet. 'The droid croaked it.' He laughed, a throaty, attractive laugh.

Ellery smiled. *This was a handsome man,* they thought, *straight nose, clear skin and piercing blue eyes. One of us could be tempted.*

'Do you do sex on a first meet?' asked Ellery.

'I do anything you want; I'm an android, employed by the B Pod Federation to keep its employees safe and happy — oh — and also clean the drains,' he added, with a giggle.

Ellery smirked. *Not a bad way to spend a wet day*, she thought, hoping for a few more rainy days to come.

# The Visit

## Clare Martin

***a gin and tonic, for old times' sake***

It's the leaving that's hard.

Arriving's okay. Warmth, loud music from the TV lounge, the twittering of caged birds and murmured conversation. A lingering smell of gravy, a hint of polish. The sharp undertone of bleach.

Quiet and heavy – a blanket that warms, comforts and restricts.

I'm greeted with a smile and a cheerful hello from everyone I pass, as a carer takes me through. We exchange quick, elliptical remarks, filling me in on today's state of play.

And then she's there, at the end of the corridor – smile wavering, eyes spurting hot tears of mingled relief and happiness.

'Oooh hoo!' Her fingers waggle at me.

We hug – my arms trying to encompass every bit of her, conveying love, reassurance, and so-happy-to-see-you.

On a good day, I swiftly turn tears to a watery chuckle with a bit of nonsensical chatter. A silly song. Something and nothing.

On a bad day, we stand swaying together awhile, me murmuring consolation into her soft, flyaway hair until she's ready to have her arm tucked into mine and take a gentle stroll around the unit.

Correction. Her home.

We find a place to sit and talk – me willing myself to relax, sit back in my chair, and chat about the weather, the birds, the flowers, the children.

All the while, my inner self is perched on the edge of my seat, eyes scanning her face, straining to catch every last drop of her words, willing there to be meaning beneath the rote phrases. To see in her eyes some sense of self, some fleeting wisp of memory.

Those eyes. Still bright blue.

How piercing they were when she detected me in wrong-doing. How warm and loving when my actions filled her with pride.

Now behind the gaze lies blankness, as though she is staring into somewhere misty and far off. A puzzle she cannot untangle.

Time passes – more nonsense, interspersed with quick checks of her physical state. And always, always, trying to make her laugh.

It's the leaving that's hard. It kills a little bit of me, every time.

Towards the end of the afternoon, I make 'got to leave soon' noises. My gut twists as I talk of journey times, weather, hours of daylight left, where the kids are and how I have to get home to them soon.

Does she – always the carer, the organiser, the worrier – understand? Or do my words mean nothing?

I'm preparing myself for departure.

I stand and we link arms again and stroll along

the corridors, admiring the pictures on the wall, talking to the budgies, greeting the people we pass.

'Got to go now, Mum.'

Another all-embracing hug – trying to give through my whole body, my mind, my heart, anything to arm her for the coming days.

The bad days, the confused days, the past-is-here-and-now days, the pain-filled memory days.

I slide slowly towards the front door.

Look back.

There she stands, rudderless, adrift in a sea of warmth and kind, compassionate care. Yet still adrift – blue eyes un-focusing in a look of loss and leaving.

# NOVEMBER

# Why Else Do We Live?

**Dana G Nadeau**

***akpeteshie***

I lived in Nigeria in the 1970s as a volunteer teacher. My housemate was from Sri Lanka. Every few months or so we would drive in his car from the small town of Keffi to the state's capital Jos. There we could go to a real grocery store and perhaps hear a phone ring! Stay overnight in a guest house. Even go to the cinema to see a dubbed Italian Western.

The road to Jos from Keffi was dirt, a mud pit in the rainy season, a minefield of hard ruts in the dry season. It was virtually undriveable in the wet season, so one day in the dry season, we set off for Jos. It was at least a five hour drive just to cover 150 miles.

About twelve miles from Jos, our car broke down. We were in the savannah – no man's land. Two school boys appeared out of nowhere. One said there was a mechanic in a nearby village just over a nearby ridge, out of sight. The other boy went to fetch him. The mechanic came, looked under the bonnet, fiddled around for a bit, and said our car needed a new part. But that part could only be obtained in the city twelve miles away.

'Don't worry,' said one of the boys. 'I'll run to the city and fetch the part for you.' What? It's twelve miles! 'I'll return in the morning.' He was barefoot.

Snakes and scorpions lay half dead or scuttled across the road, run over by day for the snakes and hurrying at night for the scorpions. Fortunately, there was a full moon. You could read a book by the light of that moon. Off he went with the useless part. Would he be stung or bitten on the way?

As is proper and customary, we went along a narrow path up and over the ridge to the village to meet and greet the chief. It would have been a grave insult to do otherwise. He told us he would put us up for the night. The villagers all sleep on straw mats in their huts. But for us they provided an empty hut, found two folding metal beds, mattresses, mosquito nets, a tin of instant coffee (which they don't drink), a water filter (they don't filter their water), and they fed us. Where had all this stuff come from?

In the morning the young boy came running back with the part. The mechanic fit it and the car started perfectly.

We offered to pay the mechanic. No. We offered the boy money for his trouble, his twenty-four mile run. No.

I thought, *Oh, I've done the wrong thing here. We have to give something to the chief, and he will distribute it accordingly.* But, no. He also refused.

This was a very, very poor African village. The villagers tilled the hard, near barren soil with hand hoes; they had no electricity, no running water; each person had an annual income of just a few shillings.

No one seemed able to afford even a bicycle. Yet as a whole they gave us rich (compared to them) strangers all that they could to help us, things they had collected, that they didn't even use themselves.

Had I offended them? Why the refusals? In the Western world, payment is given for services rendered. 'I'm really sorry,' I said, 'if we have offended you.'

I think the chief saw my confusion. I was only twenty-seven: too young to understand until the chief explained.

He raised his hand and spoke in Hausa (which one of the boys translated).

'Why else do we live, but to help each other?'

He would accept nothing because he lived by a higher principle as did all those in the village under his guidance. Our purpose in life, he clearly believed and lived by, whatever our personal circumstance, wealthy or poor, is to help each other with no expectation of reward.

We drove to Jos with our student runner, and paid for the part. Before we could discuss his return, off he set on the twelve mile run back to his village.

We were left to remember that lesson, 'Why else do we live?'

# Red Tricycle

## Katherine Abbott

***espresso***

'Do you know you're always talking about windows?' he said.

'Am I?' I answered.

Rewinding. Everything racing; downrush. Standing in the nursery yard. Four years old. Watching the other children interact and play, being on the other side of the imaginary window, looking in. The outsider. I remember admiring it. Looking. *Why can't I do that? Why can't I interact with him?* He is the boy, the boy on the vivid, red trike. I wanted a turn, but I didn't know how to ask. So, I didn't ask. Instead, I stood and watched.

# Precious

**Stephen Bridger**

***Sauvignon Blanc***

He is as sure as any father can be that his daughter must have stolen it.

'No, Daddy, I didn't take it.'

Zia is nine. She doesn't fidget or look away. Her hazel eyes are wide open, urging him to believe. And he wants to, but there's a weird complicity here. A game she's playing as much as he is because it has to be her. If it isn't then he's lost. Up until now this possession has always been a permanent fixture.

'Oh, for heaven's sake, Jeffrey, you're obsessed!' His wife spits the last word back at him.

He knows what kind of day she has had by the way she unpeels her work shoes from her sweaty feet, or the manner in which she hugs, kisses and lifts Zia into her tired arms, or the moment she lets go and sinks, deflated into her armchair.

He boils the kettle, places the decaffeinated teabag into her favourite mug, the one with the two smiling foxes on either side.

'I expect it's where you left it.' There's a time when she would have invested more energy into her assessment of his failings. 'Men can never find anything,' she adds.

The Six O'clock News is about to start. When he

sets her mug of tea on the trestle table beside her, she barely glances up at him.

Zia has had her dinner – two fish fingers, peas, and reheated white rice – and now sits at the kitchen table, her left leg swings like the beat of a metronome, while she chews the top of her pencil and focuses on the next sum in her arithmetic exercise book. 'Do you need help?' he asks.

'No, Daddy, I don't.'

He has already searched her school bag, the side pockets of her grey uniform, the drawers of her bedside table, under her bed, under her mattress, in her odds and bobs jars on the windowsill, in her two piggy banks and in her wardrobe with the jumble of boxes containing soft toys, dolls, miniature tea sets, spirographs, a telescope, a selection of My Little Ponys and even a pink Light Sabre which had once been her favourite thing but now sits neglected next to all the other stuff she's outgrown.

'They grow up fast, don't they?' It is one of his wife's favourite expressions. He nods his agreement. 'One moment they're this high, and the next…'

Zia is their only child. He doesn't know why his wife invokes the plural to make her point. They will never be capable of having another. One cycle of IVF paid for by the NHS and the other three are not. When Zia arrives on a frosty morning in January, they both decide she's worth more than the sum of their disappointments. By then he can no longer work. Instead he has to battle through various assessments and appeals to claim his Personal Independence Payments. The princely sum of seventy-two pounds and sixty-five pence. Not much more than his hourly rate as a plumber, but spinal stenosis has put paid to fiddling with downpipes and u-bends.

He refuses to believe they are poor. They just have to make do with a little less. He stays at home. His wife works.

His father gave him the silver coin a week before he died. His voice little more than a hoarse whisper, his face emaciated, his eyes dull and lifeless. Withered fingers pressed the silver into the palm of his hand. 'Keep it,' his father said. 'It's yours now, like it was my fathers before me.'

He knows the story. They all do. Passchendaele. The third battle of Ypres. August 1917. In the trenches or some muddy hell hole, a sniper's bullet hit his grandfather full square on the chest. He would have died save for the silver shilling within his breast pocket. The coin still bears the marks of where the bullet struck. Two millimetres – the thickness of the tarnished metal – the difference between life and death. A memento handed down from grandfather to father to son.

He wouldn't be alive today without its protection – nor Zia – her life as much tied to her great grandfather's coin as it is to him.

But his wife is right. When last checked he could buy a 1916 silver shilling for barely more than the cost of a franchise latte. It shouldn't mean anything, and yet it's the last thing he touches when he leaves the house, and the first thing when he returns, a habit so ingrained that the next morning his fingers linger on the hallway shelf where it normally sits, and he pauses for its absence, filled with a strange foreboding.

'Wait, Zia. Wait!'

Her hand turns the front door handle.

'What is it, Daddy?'

'Let's have a mufti day,' he says.

'What's that?' Zia stands there, front door open, her tiny eyebrows squished together, frowning.

He's as confused as she is. Maybe his mother said this once, or his grandmother. 'It means a day where we can wear what we want, Zia. A day of… possibility.'

'But I want to go to school.'

'Not today. School is off. How about we watch TV, make pancakes…'

'But I won't see Ginni!'

'You'll see Ginni tomorrow.' But he remembers tomorrow is a Saturday and she won't and his face crumples, unsure why he is lying and why it is so important she doesn't leave the house when it's not raining, not even that cold. It's the week before half-term, eight days before Halloween and all that nonsense which comes around with wearying predictability every year. It seems so fake and yet Zia loves it.

'Promise?'

'Yes, I promise,' he replies.

While she is changing out of her uniform, he phones the school.

'I hope she's better soon,' the school secretary says.

'I'm sure she'll be back by Monday,' he replies.

He makes Zia a hot chocolate, and then lets her watch cartoons on the TV while he carries out another search of their house. He goes through every pocket in every pair of trousers, even those he hasn't worn in years. And when she tires of television, they play a game of treasure hunt – he has secreted half a dozen mini chocolate bars from a variety bag bought for the Trick Or Treaters. Zia greets each new discovery with a shriek of joy, but the only thing of importance remains unclaimed.

There's the occasional muffled sound of sirens but no more than usual, and when he checks the local news reports there are no reported accidents. No acts of violence. Just the usual Friday morning in South London.

He is being an idiot. He has overreacted. But when Zia asks to go to the park, he says no.

'You said we could do anything!' Chocolate smears her lips, her left cheek, her fingers.

He wipes her protesting face with a Jay Cloth. 'You know what, why don't we try out your Halloween costume? We'll surprise Mummy when she comes home. How about that?'

This endless negotiation exhausts him, and he's not good at it. *Is he a bad father?* But his doubts run deeper than making Zia stay at home when she should be at school. He loves her – of course, he does – but is that enough? He has always compared himself to others – other parents, other relatives – who laugh and chat as if this were the most natural thing in the world, but it isn't. For him. He's older. He walks with a stick. The spinal stenosis and surgeries have reaped their toll on his failing body. Getting anywhere takes effort, energy and will, and the supply of each is dwindling.

Sometimes he wonders whether the tension between the three of them is a product of the way Zia arrived in this world. An unnatural occurrence when nature and the natural order decreed otherwise. It's a stupid thought, made stupider by the fact he wouldn't have it any other way but his bond with Zia is fragile. He witnesses this fragility in a thousand ways – and the older she gets, the more he considers that one day their connection will break and she will drift away as if there was nothing between them.

He wants her to grow up. He wants her to have the chances and choices denied to him but at the same time – and this is the contradiction he holds tightly within himself – he wants the Zia whose whole world can be encompassed by his arms. But now she has Ginni, Emma and Francine and too many others of whom he isn't even aware of.

There is a world growing outside of him. A world he will never know. Soon she will have other friends. And boys, and what will he mean to her then? A dutiful call? A filial act of obligation?

His wife returns home with a plastic carrier containing a bottle of Sauvignon Blanc still cold from the supermarket refrigerator, and a party sized bag of cheese and onion crisps. She swings their daughter who is now cloaked in her witches' garb in a wide arc around the kitchen. Zia whoops in delight, her hat flies to the floor, her feet narrowly miss the nearest of the kitchen chairs.

'How was school today?'

'I didn't go to school, mummy. We had a mufti day!'

It takes a little explaining. He'll tell the truth later.

He reheats his wife's favourite lamb curry which they eat with rice and two different jars of shop bought chutneys. All three of them sit at the kitchen table. This is the first time they have sat together this week.

'What are we celebrating?' he asks when he's pouring them both a glass of wine.

'Oh, nothing,' his wife replies. 'I just thought… I deserved it.'

Three weeks later, Half Term and Halloween over, the coin still missing – not forgotten, but he's learning to accept its absence as a new normal, something he will tolerate because he has no choice but to. And he has to acknowledge that despite his fears – irrational as he now admits – nothing bad has happened to him or Zia. 'And nothing will,' his wife assures him when he confesses. He expects her to laugh or scream, but instead she smiles – a weak, half smile – and places her hand on his shoulder as if he needs support. 'I didn't realise you were so superstitious. You didn't think that coin was lucky, did you?'

Zia has written her usual wish list to a Santa whom she no longer believes in, while he accumulates the required yuletide stuff – a snow globe (she always has a snow globe), scented candles, glittery wrapping paper, Christmas crackers – counting every penny as he negotiates needs and wants in Poundland and the Charity shops, but there is an item he cannot find – a calendar with pictures of her favourite singer from her recent world tour. It is enough to drive him half mad hunting for something which should be there but isn't. In the end, he has to ask his wife.

'It's thirteen pounds and ninety-eight pence,' she says. 'Daylight robbery!'

'Can I have a look?' He holds out his hand.

She flicks her eyebrows to the heavens, but hands him her phone.

'Do you want tea?' She pushes herself up from her chair.

He shakes his head and scrolls. There are over 400,000 results related to her search – Amazon, Etsy, the official Taylor Swift domains and many others –

but most aren't for calendars. Many are not even related to the singer, but at the bottom of the screen there's an offer on eBay for under a tenner. He clicks on this link, taps impatiently on the side of his chair for the site to open. It's his wife's eBay account. He knows it's wrong but cannot resist the opportunity to see what she last bought. Instead the screen opens at her selling history. It's there. The King's head in half profile, his left ear blurred and blunted from the imprint of the German bullet. *George V DEI GRA: BRITT: OMNI: REX* inscribed around its circumference. His silver coin. Sold for the cost of a calendar. Or a cheap bottle of wine and a packet of crisps.

He stabs at the X on the top right of the screen, places the phone on the table beside his wife's chair and presses both his shaking hands hard into his thighs. The spinal stenosis has numbed his legs but there's still a faint echo of pain where his fingers squeeze withered flesh.

'Did you find a better deal?' his wife asks on her return. One of the foxes grins at him as she places her mug on the coaster.

'Yes,' he replies. 'It's cheaper on eBay.'

'Oh, is it? That's good. Well, I'll get it then, shall I?'

'Yes, dear. If you don't mind.'

# DECEMBER

# Nothing Left to Know

**Mike Lee**

***sparkling water***

Dave entered community college after the registrar volunteered to review his high school transcript.

When Dave handed the transcript to the clerk, he was told to go to 'that man' first. Since he was a dropout and had yet to take his general equivalency diploma, Dave needed his approval to register at the community college.

The registrar looked at the sheet, sighed, and mumbled, 'Okaaaayyyy.'

Upon handing it back to him, he said, 'Perfect grades in Philosophy and Religion, Media Studies and the histories. You flunked nearly every other class.'

He paused. 'You're either going somewhere important – or waking up in the morning under an overpass. It's your choice, now.'

This was on an afternoon during the late summer heat. Dave had sold his collection of punk rock singles at a used record shop before heading to the auditorium for class registration.

Dave remembered the man's gaze when he handed back his transcript. They locked eyes.

The registrar hesitated for a moment before letting it go from his grasp.

He looked hopeful, or so Dave believed, as he turned away from him to get back into the registration line.

'Good luck,' the man said as Dave walked away.

Dave sighed in relief, paid his fees, and bought his textbooks with the money he had earned from selling the singles.

Dave registered for four classes: Sociology, Introduction to Psychology, an introductory course in English Literature, and Texas History. Three classes were held at the old high school building at Rio Grande Street, and Texas History was an at-home study, with classroom dates to turn in midterms and final papers.

Two weeks after classes began, he got a job a mile from the school washing dishes at a steak house, four nights a week, at minimum wage.

The job was repetitive and mindless, and it made him feel at ease. The rhythm of shoving racks, pressing the button on the Auto-Chlor dishwasher, and putting dishes and trays away gave him opportunities to daydream while Tony, the main cook, blasted Delta blues and obscure old country music from the radio cassette deck combo on the steel rack next to the grille.

During downtime, Dave studied and read the Diamond Sutra, trying to make sense of its heavily fathomed depths.

A month into the job, Dave saved enough to move from home. Since he didn't have a car, it became too embarrassing to drive to school and work.

Mom didn't mind. She told him she could use the emotional space.

So did he.

He found a notice on the bulletin board at the liquor store down the block from work advertising a garden studio behind one of the houses around the corner. It was furnished at $150 a month, and utilities were paid.

The studio was a converted shed. Its kitchenette featured a 1920s double sink with chrome and glass touches. It was furnished with an aged fold-out couch, a coffee table, and a single bed. Dave did his homework at the red Formica dining table, listening to music on his cassette player.

Leona, his landlady, lived in the main house. She was friendly and occasionally doted on him. Dave helped with her garden on Sundays, and sometimes they dined together.

So this was home. His telephone was in the booth outside the liquor store. Dave called his mother daily to let her know he was okay. Now and then, she didn't pick up, but he learned not to mind.

He didn't hang out as much with his friends, and outside of a visit by a couple of them shortly after he moved in, only his landlady and from time to time his mother came by. He enjoyed the solitude, studying with his textbooks and reading books such as the Dhammapada, the Sutras, Alan Watts, and others.

One morning in November, when the heat

dissipated into autumn cool, he arrived early to study in the high school's former cafeteria. It was repurposed into a common area, with snack machines and a rack of video games in the back.

He just sat down when he felt a tap on his shoulder.

'Whoa.'

Standing over him was a guise from the near past. Sherry was one of his ex-girlfriend's friends. Her peroxide hair was stuffed in a Greek Fisherman's cap, and under her bomber jacket, she wore a Joy Division T-shirt.

'Hey! Nice running into you,' she said. 'I heard you were here. How've you been?'

'Fine,' Dave said. He was sheepish about talking to her, given she was close to his ex-girlfriend. That relationship didn't end well.

She pointed at the stack of books next to his open spiral. 'That can't all be for your classes?'

'No, not really. Been reading a lot since the summer,' he said. 'I guess I will read until there is nothing left to know.'

They chatted for a short time. Sherry was taking a Math Intro class to fulfil her obligations at the university, and she was still making the music scene. Dave was reticent about the past but listened to the gossip. Monica, his ex, was dating a bass player.

What is around him is noise except for the flip of the page, and a pen scratching on lined paper.

He thought of Alan Watts's writing about change

and joining the dance. Dave was, as far as he was concerned, dancing well.

Sherry had to leave for class and promised to meet next Thursday. After watching her leave, Dave returned to writing in his notebook, beginning his morning ritual of creating form out of desire.

Thursday, he wrote. Thursday, there is someone I want to know.

# Elf on the Shelf

## Sally Storr

*hot chocolate and cookies*

Sophie and I are enjoying a cup of tea and a mince-pie, before Izzie and Max get dropped off from yet another Christmas party.

'Why's he called Elf on the shelf? Has he been unlucky in love?' asks Granny.

'What? No, SHE sits on the shelf and interesting, educational things happen for the kids each day.' responds Sophie.

'I see. No longer "naughty or nice" then?' Granny adds.

'It's the way we do things now. We don't want our kids to feel bad – it helps them psychologically if the elf is seen as a friend.'

'I guess it's more woke is it? What's SHE done today then?'

'Well, sometimes they get a lovely toy but today it's a craft activity. She's just spelt out their names on the kitchen table in breakfast cereal,' informs Sophie.

'And that's OK is it? I mean those fruity loopy things aren't cheap. And now they can spill them all over the place as though that's a good thing!'

'You just aren't getting it are you, Mum?'

Best leave that argument to one side. Granny sighs.

'And when would you like us to give the children their presents? Christmas afternoon?'

'I don't want them feeling overwhelmed. They will have loads to open on Christmas Day and the build-up is always so knackering. They're already up every morning at 5 am…'

'So, what you're saying is you don't want our gifts?' *Oh, here we go again*, thinks Granny.

'No, no, not at all. I want to spread it out for them, so could you come Boxing Day afternoon. We've got the other grandparents coming in the morning.'

Crikey, thinks Granny. Wonder why we bother?

'I've followed all the Web links you sent me for the presents so at least you know what they're getting.'

There's a loud slam of the front door, before the children rush into the lounge, looking rather red and dishevelled.

'Granny!' they both gasp and come to give her a kiss.

'Gosh, what's that smell?' asks Granny.

'It's my cinnamon-scented glop. Look it can go everywhere,' says Max, trailing some green sludgy stuff down his clothes and onto the coffee table.

'Isn't it yummy?' he says, as Granny covers her nose and mouth with a hankie.

'Lovely dear,' she says.

'I like your Christmas pullover, Granny,' says

Izzie. 'I saw those in Tesco's the other day. Half-price.'

'Hmmmm,' says Granny. She was hoping for a few compliments on her on-trend outfit.

'So what's the agenda for the weekend?' she asks Sophie, expecting a list of Christmas activities.'

'Well, we've got the light trail tomorrow evening.'

'With marshmallows on sticks to melt over a camp fire,' adds Izzie.

'And the Polar Express train on Sunday,' says Max. 'I can't wait to wear my PJs on the train. And there's hot chocolate and cookies.'

'That sounds exciting. Where does it go? I can't imagine the North Pole around here.' Granny laughs.

'It doesn't GO anywhere,' says Sophie. 'You travel up and down a train track but it's not about the destination, it's about the journey. It's all singing, dancing and fun on the train.'

'Oh, I see. That sounds… interesting.' Granny can't think of the right adjective.

Granny thinks how different Christmas is these days.

'We had advent calendars when I was a little girl. But all you got was a Christmassy picture for each day, and a really big picture of baby Jesus on the $25^{th}$.'

'What? No chocolates?' asks Izzie. 'Sounds so boring.'

'The highlight of Christmas Day after the presents

and lunch was watching Morecambe and Wise on the telly,' says Granny. 'I wonder what you'll be doing.'

'I feel sick,' suddenly announces Max. He's clinging on to the Christmas tree as he speaks. And before anyone can do anything he pulls it towards himself and vomits at the same time. The tree and the boy both fall down, taking the lights and Christmas bunting with him. He is hardly visible under the heap.

'Yuk!' says Izzie. 'I told you not to eat any more Haribos. He had thousands Mummy.'

Sophie and Granny are rushing about trying to calm Max's tears and clear up the mess, which has managed to spread all over the floor as well as the Christmas decorations.

Sky TV suddenly pipes up for no reason at top volume.

'Let it go. Let it go,' that ubiquitous song is playing.

'Oh lovely, a vintage movie,' says Izzie, oblivious to the chaos around her.

'Granny. Do you want to watch it with me? Did they have this in the old days when you were a little girl?'

'Thank you, Izzie. I'm just helping Mummy clean up. I'll join you in a mo.'

'I'll best get Max into the shower Mum,' suggests Sophie as she carries a crying mess of a little boy out of the lounge.

'Oh, lovely. Peace and quiet,' says Izzie. 'We can relax now. Christmas is SO tiring.' says Izzie.

# Wandering Teeth

Madeleine McDonald

***horlicks***

'Bloody relatives!' The manager banged the phone down. 'That was Betty Turner's son. He's one of them. Doesn't come near the place all year round but gets an attack of conscience at Christmas and decides to visit.'

'Oh! What about—'

'Exactly. What about her teeth!'

Charlie Chaplin, the care home cat, chose that moment to pad into the office. 'Out, Charlie,' the manager ordered, without malice. 'Unless you can tell us where to find those teeth.'

Betty's dentures had been missing for a week. She had developed the unfortunate habit of removing both the upper and lower plates and putting them on the table while she ate, although her table companion Cora complained loudly that this was unhygienic. Betty countered by pointing out that Cora cleaned her reading glasses with the same handkerchief she used to blow her nose. The two women had struck up a companionship of sorts in the care home, largely based on sniping at each other's habits.

The overworked and underpaid staff took little notice. The ones who stayed in the job learned to accept the residents' various versions of reality, and to work around their foibles. They also learned to let distress and grievances go in one ear and out the other. Too much compassion led to burnout. Mealtimes were a matter of routine, so long as each resident was seen to eat something, and so long as the awkward customers did not throw food on the floor or at each other.

What usually happened was that the carer who cleared away the dirty plates wrapped Betty's teeth in a paper napkin and returned them to the wash glass in her bedroom. This time, no-one remembered having done so.

Cora kept quiet. She had taken the dentures to teach Betty a lesson, but had no real idea where to hide them until she spotted the Christmas tree. As always, it took pride of place in the residents' lounge, a reminder to many of happier times. A carer hurried across the room when she saw Cora fiddling with the strands of tinsel wound in and out of its green branches. 'Cora, love, let's leave the pretty decorations for everyone to enjoy. What have you got there?'

Cora opened her hand to reveal a felt reindeer minus one antler. The carer dropped it into her pocket and settled Cora back in a chair. She failed to notice Betty's upper plate, gleaming pink and cream among the profusion of fairy lights, tinsel and sparkly decorations.

Delighted with her own cunning, Cora forgot about the lower plate, which was still in her trouser pocket when the carers collected the week's washing.

Charlie Chaplin got the blame, as he got the blame for many minor incidents. 'What have you done with Betty's teeth, you naughty cat?' The question was rhetorical, a way for the carers to acknowledge his presence as they went about their work.

With his glossy black coat, white shirt front and white paws, Charlie Chaplin was a firm favourite with residents and staff. Oak Tree Lodge had once been a grand Victorian villa, but an extension built in the 1980s had doubled its size. Charlie patrolled both parts of his territory tail held high, slipping out at night to hunt mice in what was left of the garden.

During the day, he headbutted his favourite residents on their ankles and left black and white hairs over all the cushions. Both manager and staff felt that vacuuming up a few hairs was a small price to pay for putting a smile on the residents' faces.

Many residents led confused, resentful lives, abandoned by relatives who could not cope with their decline. For some, Charlie was the only living being who showed them affection. Like Annie, who so wanted to keep busy 'helping' the care staff. Usually, they asked her to dust the windowsills of the entrance hall, which she did, back and forth, over and over again. Unless she encountered Charlie sunning himself on one of the window ledges. Then she tickled his ears and talked to him. Charlie flicked his tail in acknowledgement.

He found an enemy in Ms Miller, the new cook. Ms Miller had graduated from catering college with top marks; the manager lost no time in placing her photo and certificates in a prominent position on the home's display board. Apart from a genuine love of food, Ms Miller had a passion for cleanliness, leading by example and scrubbing the kitchen equipment to within an inch of its life. 'I want that floor clean enough to eat off before you go home,' she barked at her team. They obeyed, grudgingly, but since no-one could accuse her of idleness, the grumbles were muted.

In theory, the manager and her staff agreed with the requirement for scrupulous hygiene, but life had taught them to turn a blind eye to some regulations if that kept the residents comfortable. Good cheer was too much to hope for, but a comfortable atmosphere eased the load on the staff. The manager knew certain residents enticed Charlie into their bedrooms, and even up onto their beds, although the rules forbade it. She made sure Ms Miller's diktats stopped at the kitchen door.

Until the night Charlie Chaplin found the kitchen door open. Betty's upper denture had fallen out of the Christmas tree in the lounge right under his nose. The smell was irresistible and Charlie worried at it like prey, rolling it over and batting it along the corridor.

Somewhere a door banged. Stopped in his tracks,

Charlie's ears swivelled. The wind rattled the windows, but the house remained sunk in slumber. Charlie followed a new, enticing smell to the door of forbidden territory. The scent was all the more enticing for that, and he squeezed his lithe body through the now open door.

With a leap onto the counter worktop, he discovered a chicken carcase that had been left to cool under a mesh dome. He knocked dome and plate onto the floor, on top of the teeth.

What were plastic teeth compared to succulent chicken bones? Charlie crunched, nibbled, slept, and nibbled again.

The first person to arrive in the kitchen the next morning was a trainee. By now Charlie was digesting his feast in the residents' lounge, and all she saw in her panic was a broken plate and scattered bones. She scooped up the bones and set them on another plate. A quick mop of the floor and all appeared normal. No need to report the unfortunate accident to that pernickety Ms Miller. She would only make a tremendous fuss and want to fill in an incident form. Besides, didn't she always boast you could eat off her floors?

Thus Betty's upper plate, trapped under the chicken's breastbone, found its way into nourishing, homemade soup. Despite her martinet tendencies, Ms Miller knew the art of using up leftovers, and conjured up tasty dishes on a limited budget. It was one of the reasons the manager put up with her.

Ladled out by a distracted member of the care staff, Betty's denture plate plopped into Priscilla's soup bowl. As ill luck would have it, Priscilla decided the teeth looked sparkly clean – as indeed they did after simmering for hours in chicken broth. When no-one was looking, Priscilla swapped the sparkly white teeth for her own yellowing ones. They did not quite fit, but that did not matter. She admired herself in the mirror every day and the carers were too busy to notice that her top and bottom teeth no longer matched.

On the other hand, they beamed with relief on reuniting Betty with both dentures. 'Betty, love, we found them!' True, Betty's teeth were no longer the same colour but that was not surprising when the upper plate had been found in a soup bowl and the lower plate had been through a hot wash.

'There's a poltergeist at work,' one carer declared. 'Something has disturbed the spirits in the old house. There will be more trouble, you'll see.' But she was known for the doom-laden interpretation of her own daily horoscope, which she downloaded in the tea break and read aloud, so the other carers took no notice. Some happenings were destined to remain a mystery.

Poor Betty could only mumble that her teeth did not fit properly, but the staff patted her hand and moved on. Betty's family made little sense of her mumbling either, and their Christmas visit did not last long. Betty's face crumpled with distress and her rheumy eyes filled with tears.

'Bloody relatives,' the care home manager huffed as she locked the security door behind them. 'One visit a year, and he thinks that gives him the right to interrogate me like he's the Spanish Inquisition. Try doing the job 365 days a year, sonny.' She paused to compose her own ruffled feathers before scooping up Charlie Chaplin and placing him on Betty's lap. 'Look, here's Charlie come to say hello. You know how much he likes you.'

Charlie Chaplin, his crime unpunished, purred a greeting. Betty, recalling the warm weight of long-deceased pets, stroked him in silence. If she did not attempt to talk, her teeth felt almost comfortable.

# About the Authors

**Katherine Abbott**

Katherine Abbott is a working-class writer, currently pursuing a PhD in creative writing. Her stories focus on the tapestry of human experience, characterized by the perpetual search for connection, meaning, and understanding in ordinary life.

**Justin Aylward**

Justin Aylward is a writer from Co. Dublin, Ireland. He has published short fiction, poetry, a novel, and film criticism for numerous online film outlets. He is currently writing a three-act play inspired by the current fuel crisis in Europe.

**Michael Barrington**

Michael Barrington has written eight historical novels. *Passage to Murder* is a thriller set in San Francisco. *Magic at Stonehenge* is a short story collection. *Take a Priest Like You* is a memoir. He has published more than 60 short stories and also blogs on his website: www.mbwriter.net.

**Jim Bates**

Jim is an award-winning author who lives in a small town in Minnesota. He loves to write! His stories and poems have appeared in over five hundred online and print publications. He has also authored twenty-three books the most recent of which is *The Time Traveling Healer*, available through traditional outlets.

Additional stories can be found on his blog: www.theviewfromlonglake.wordpress.com.

**Stephen Bridger**

Stephen Bridger is a former hospital doctor and fledgling writer. Two of his stories were shortlisted in writing competitions, both of which led to publication (*The Bardsy Anthology 2023* and *Fish Anthology 2024*). He was longlisted (a finalist) in two categories of the Page Turner Awards in 2023. He has had other stories published in *CaféLit* and *Manifest Station.*

**Lynn Clement**

Lynn is a regular writer for CaféLit, and has had several stories published. Her first flash fiction, short story and poetry collection, *The City of Stories*, is published by Chapeltown books: #thecityofstories'.

Lynn is pleased to have had stories selected for, '*The Best of CaféLit* – 11, 12, 13 and now 14. She has won several local competitions and is trying to pluck up the courage to enter national ones.

**Niall Crowley**

Niall Crowley works on equality and human rights. His fiction is published by *CaféLit, The Galway Review, Spillwords, Pure Slush* and *The Writers Club.* He was shortlisted for the From the Well short story competition in 2021, 2022, and 2023, and the Colm Toibín International short story award in 2022.

**Kate Durrant**

The editor of two regional publications in Ireland, Kate is a regular contributor to RTE Radio One, BBC Radio Two, *Irish Farmers Journal* and co-host of the *Natter* podcast with author Michelle McDonagh.

An award winning short story writer and poet, her work has been widely published and she is currently looking forward to the publication of her first novel.

**Steve Gerson**

Steve Gerson writes poetry and flash about life's dissonance. He has published in *CaféLit*, *Panoplyzine*, *Decadent Review*, *Vermilion*, *In Parentheses* and more, plus his six chapbooks: *Once Planed Straight*, *Viral*, *And the Land Dreams Darkly*, *The 13th Floor: Step into Anxiety*, *What Is Isn't* and *There Is a Season*.

**Elise Glassman**

Elise Glassman is a neuro-divergent, New Orleans-based writer published by *The Colorado Review, Main Street Rag, The Portland Review,* and *Per Contra*. She is as an assistant fiction editor for Pithead Chapel, and greatly appreciates the time and care CaféLit gives to submissions.

**Monica Goertzen Hertlein**

Monica always wanted to write, but never thought it was a real job. After career and family, she returned to her passion of fiction writing. She has been published in *Impulse*, *Embark*, *Swords & Sorceries: Tales of Heroic Fantasy Volume 8*, *AnotherRealm* and *The Lorelei*

*Signal.* She grew up, resides, and writes in Saskatoon, Saskatchewan, Canada on Treaty 6 Territory and the homeland of the Métis.

www.monicagh.com

**Sandra Horn**

Sandra's family in Bristol, Scotland and New Zealand, provide huge inspiration for her stories, which appear in national women's magazines. Otherwise, she writes of the supernatural or with a sinister twist, and about bigger issues such as child abuse. She has won several competitions, and has been included in an erotic anthology.

**Claire Jaggard**

Claire lives in South Gloucestershire, works as a journalist and writes for pleasure. Her stories have been longlisted, shortlisted and published by Stroud Short Stories, appeared in online publications and broadcast by BBC Upload. She's currently researching ways to commit murder for her first cosy mystery.

https://clairejaggard.com

**Gill James**

Gill James is published by The Red Telephone, Butterfly and Chapeltown. She edits CaféLit and writes for the online community news magazine: Talking About My Generation. She teaches Creative Writing and has an MA in Writing for Children and PhD in Creative and Critical Writing.

www.gilljameswriter.com

**Maria Kinnersley**

Maria started writing having left her job in local government due to ill health. Her stories have appeared in two anthologies. She has also published non-fiction articles, and she is currently working on a collection of short stories. Her home is in Devon.

**Olof Laamanen**

Olof Laamanen is a retired computer engineer. He's a newcomer to fiction writing, and specializes in romance novellas. None of them have so far been published. *Reminiscences* is his first short story.

Swedish is his native language, and English is his third.

**Mike Lee**

Mike Lee's work appears in or is forthcoming in *CaféLit, Drunk Monkeys*, and others. In addition, his story collection, *The Northern Line*, is available on online bookselling outlets. He was also nominated for Best Microfiction by Ghost Parachute.

**Henry Lewi**

Henry is a retired surgeon and a member of the Canvey Writers Group.

He has published a number of stories on the CaféLit site.

**Peter Lingard**

Peter Lingard sold ice-cream, worked as a bank clerk, a bookkeeper, and a barman. He served in the Royal Marines and owned a freight forwarding company in New York. He went to Australia because the sun frequently shines there and he didn't have to learn the language. His published novels are *Boswell's Fairies* and *The Book of Dave.* He has a collection of short stories published under the title *Ruffians, Rogues and Romantics.*

**Clare Martin**

Clare Martin is a writer with a background in radio journalism. Based in Sussex, England, she specialises in flash fiction and short stories. Writing about what lies under the surface of ordinary life, she draws inspiration from overheard conversations and the tales we tell ourselves.

**Madeleine McDonald**

Madeleine McDonald lives on the Yorkshire coast, where beach walks provide thinking time. In 2024 she won the Table/FEAST fiction prize for writers aged 50+. As befits a former précis-writer, she enjoys the challenge of micro-fiction, and in 2024 had a 53-word story published in *What Dwells Between the Lines*, as well as two 42-word stories in the *Book of $42^2$*. Her historical novel, *A Shackled Inheritance*, is available on Amazon Kindle.

**Mia McNamara**

Mia McNamara is a young author in college who has been writing since 2015. She is currently eighteen years old and is looking for ways to expand her work so her name can become known.

**Rob Molan**

Rob lives in Edinburgh and started writing short stories during the pandemic. A number of his tales have been published in anthologies and on websites. He loves the challenge of identifying an idea for a tale and turning it into a narrative which engages readers.

**Jane Mooney**

Jane Mooney writes short stories and children's fiction in the beautiful Pennine hills in Yorkshire, England. She was longlisted in the *Searchlight Children's Picture Book Text 2024* competition. Her short stories have been published by *Funny Pearls*, *CaféLit*, *Pure Slush* and *The People's Friend.*

**Linda Morse**

Linda has written four full-length plays and has had short plays and monologues performed in venues across the West Country and London. Work has recently been completed on her short film, Happy Hour.

**Dana G Nadeau**

Born in Long Beach, California, but grew up in Lancaster, Pennsylvania, Dana has lived in Nigeria, West Africa, done a post-grad degree in English and American Lit at Leeds Uni, taught in Switzerland, become a British citizen, served as a magistrate, and now lives in Accrington, Lancashire. She has published a novel *The Cloven Pine* which has received very good reviews.

**Hannah Retallick**

Hannah Retallick is from Anglesey, North Wales. She was home educated and then studied with the Open University, graduating with a first-class BA (Honours) Arts and Humanities (Creative Writing and Music) degree, before passing her creative writing MA with distinction. Her work has gained success in several international competitions.

**Judith Skilleter**

Judith Skilleter is new to writing fiction after a long career in social work and teaching and her first children's novel will be published shortly. She is a Geordie, who settled in East Yorkshire forty-five years ago and is married with four grandchildren.

**Sally Storr**

Sally Storr is a psychologist and works as a coach. She has always been equally fascinated by human behaviour and by figures from literature. She's been writing all her life but especially enjoys writing about quirky things that happen to ordinary people like herself.

**Laura Sukonick**

At thirty-six years old Laura lives with her husband, her two cats, and her existential dread. In her spare time she enjoys reflecting on the often ineffective ways that she's tried to deal with the hassle of being herself. For the last decade she's worked as a psychotherapist.

**Rick Vick**

Sadly Rick died before *Ways of Seeing* was complete. Steven John, who represented Rick in the editorial process, wrote in his introduction to the book: 'Rick saw no difference between, and spoke no differently to, the homeless person sleeping rough in the doorway or the well-to-do visitor to the art gallery or poetry reading holding a complimentary glass of wine. During his life in Stroud, he was involved in social work, leading creative writing classes for ex-offenders and those with addiction issues.'

**Frank Zahn**

Frank Zahn is an author of fiction, nonfiction, and poetry. His publications include nonfiction books, articles, commentaries, book reviews, and essays; novels; short stories; and poetry. Currently, he writes and enjoys life at his home among the evergreens in Vancouver, Washington. For details, visit his website, www.frankzahn.com

# Index of Drinks

## Like to Read More Work Like This?

Then sign up to our mailing list and download our free collection of short stories, *Magnetism*. Sign up now to receive this free e-book and also to find out about all of our new publications and offers.

Sign up here:
http://eepurl.com/gbpdVz

## Please Leave a Review

Reviews are so important to writers. Please take the time to review this book. A couple of lines is fine.

Reviews help the book to become more visible to buyers. Retailers will promote books with multiple reviews.

This in turn helps us to sell more books… And then we can afford to publish more books like this one.

Leaving a review is very easy.

Go to https://amzn.to/4ksnTNg, scroll down the left-hand side of the Amazon page and click on the 'Write a customer review' button.

# Writing for CaféLit

Have you got a story in you? Do you think it would suit CaféLit?

We're looking for thought-provoking and entertaining stories, though ones which might be a tad different from what you normally read in a woman's magazine. They should be the sort of length that would make easy reading whilst you drink a cup of coffee, even if you linger a while, but without you needing to rent a table.

So, no more than 3000 words. Shorter stories and flash fiction are naturally very welcome.

We'll read your story. If we like it, we'll let you know and if we don't like it we'll let you know – within a month. We will work on editing with you.

Each year we'll publish a volume of the best stories. If you are in the volume you will have a share of the profits.

Our editing process will also include some work on your bio to maximise its effect.

We also ask you assign your story the name of a drink. Something light and frothy might be a hot chocolate. A dark piece of flash fiction could be an espresso. Something good for the soul would be a mint tea.

Full submission details can be found at

www.cafelit.co.uk/index.php/submission-guidelines-2.

# Also by Chapeltown Books

## 'The Best of CaféLit' series

Each story in these little volumes is the right length and quality for enjoying as you sip the assigned drink in your favourite Creative Café.

Order from Amazon:

CaféLit 2011
ISBN: 978-0-9568680-3-9 (paperback) 978-0-9568680-4-6 (ebook)
CaféLit 2012
ISBN: 978-0-9568680-8-4 (paperback) 978-0-9568680-9-1 (ebook)
CaféLit 3
ISBN: 978-1-910542-00-2 (paperback) 978-1-910542-01-9 (ebook)
CaféLit 4
ISBN: 978-1-910542-02-6 (paperback) 978-1-910542-03-3 (ebook)
CaféLit 5
ISBN: 978-1-910542-04-0 (paperback) 978-1-910542-05-7 (ebook)
CaféLit 6
ISBN: 978-1-910542-17-0 (paperback) 978-1-910542-18-7 (ebook)
CaféLit 7
ISBN: 978-1-910542-40-8 (paperback) 978-1-910542-41-5 (ebook)
CaféLit 8
ISBN: 978-1-910542-45-3 (paperback) 978-1-910542-46-0 (ebook)
CaféLit 9
ISBN: 978-1-910542-54-5 (paperback) 978-1-910542-55-2 (ebook)
CaféLit 10
ISBN: 978-1-910542-76-7 (paperback) 978-1-910542-77-4 (ebook)
CaféLit 11
ISBN: 978-1-910542-89-7 (paperback) 978-1-910542-90-3 (ebook)
CaféLit 12
ISBN: 978-1-915762-03-0 (paperback) 978-1-915762-04-7 (ebook)
CaféLit 13
ISBN: 978-1-915762-10-8 (paperback) 978-1-915762-11-5 (ebook)

**Chapeltown Books**

Printed in Dunstable, United Kingdom

63611345R00127